Praise for John D. MacDonald

'The Dickens of mid-century America – popular, prolific and … conscience-ridden about his environment … a thoroughly American author.'

—*The Boston Globe*

'It will be for his crisply written, smoothly plotted mysteries that MacDonald will be remembered.'

—*USA Today*

'In McGee mysteries and other novels as well, MacDonald's voice was one of a social historian.'

—*Los Angeles Times*

'MacDonald had the marvelous ability to create attention-getting characters who doubled as social critics. In MacDonald novels, it is the rule rather than the exception to find, in the midst of violence and mayhem, a sentence, a paragraph, or several pages of rumination on love, morality, religion, architecture, politics, business, the general state of the world or of Florida.'

—Sarasota *Herald-Tribune*

By John D. MacDonald
(published in The Murder Room)

The Brass Cupcake (1950)
Murder for the Bride (1951)
The Neon Jungle (1953)
Cancel All Our Vows (1953)
Area of Suspicion (1954)
Contrary Pleasure (1954)
A Bullet for Cinderella (1955) (aka *On the Make*)
Cry Hard, Cry Fast (1956)
April Evil (1956)
Border Town Girl (1956) (aka *Five Star Fugitive*)
Murder in the Wind (1956) (aka *Hurricane*)
You Live Once (1956) (aka *You Kill Me*)
Death Trap (1957)
The Price of Murder (1957)
A Man of Affairs (1957)
The Deceivers (1958)
Soft Touch (1958)
Deadly Welcome (1959)
The Beach Girls (1959)
Please Write for Details (1959)
The Crossroads (1959)
Slam the Big Door (1960)
The Only Girl in the Game (1960)
The End of the Night (1960)
Where is Janice Gantry? (1961)
One Monday We Killed Them All (1961)
A Key to the Suite (1962)
A Flash of Green (1962)
I Could Go On Singing (screenplay novelisation) (1963)
On the Run (1963)
The Drowner (1963)
The Last One Left (1966)
No Deadly Drug (1968)
One More Sunday (1984)
Barrier Island (1986)

COLLECTIONS

The Good Old Stuff (1961)
Seven (1971)
More Good Old Stuff (1984)

John D. MacDonald (1916–1986) is one of the world's bestselling novelists. He began his writing career after serving in the Army from 1940 to 1946. He started by penning stories for pulp magazines and then published his first novel, *The Brass Cupcake*, in 1950. In 1972, he was recognised by the Mystery Writers of America as a Grand Master for lifetime achievement. At the time of his death, he had published seventy-eight books, close to five hundred short stories, and had seen about seventy-five million copies of his works in print.

CAPE FEAR

Originally published as
The Executioners

John D. MacDonald

An Orion paperback

First published in Great Britain in 1957
by John D. MacDonald Publishing, Inc.
This paperback edition published in 2014
by Orion Books,
an imprint of The Orion Publishing Group Ltd,
Orion House, 5 Upper St Martin's Lane,
London WC2H 9EA

An Hachette UK company

A CIP catalogue record for this book is available from the British Library.

Typeset by Input Data Services Ltd, Bridgwater, Somerset

Printed and bound by CPI Group (UK) Ltd, Croydon, CR0 4YY

The Orion Publishing Group's policy is to use papers that are natural, renewable and recyclable products and made from wood grown in sustainable forests. The logging and manufacturing processes are expected to conform to the environmental regulations of the country of origin.

www.orionbooks.co.uk

For Howard, who believed;
and for Jennie, who believed in Howard

CHAPTER ONE

Sam Bowden lay on his back under a high Saturday sun, eyes closed, right hand clasping the fading chill of half a can of beer. He was aware of the nearness of Carol. Digestion of the picnic lunch was proceeding comfortably. Jamie and Bucky were thrashing around in the brush on the small hill behind the little beach, and Sam knew it would soon be time for eleven-year-old Jamie to send six-year-old Bucky down to them to ask if it wasn't time to go back into the water. Other years Nancy would have been racing and whooping with the younger kids.

But this year Nancy was fourteen, and this year she had brought a guest along – a fifteen-year-old boy named Pike Foster. Nancy and Pike lay baking in the sun on the foredeck of the *Sweet Sioux III*, with a portable radio turned to the odd offerings of a progressive disk jockey. The *Sweet Sioux* was moored a hundred feet down the curve of beach, her bow ten feet off the sand, and the music was barely audible.

Sam Bowden lay with the sun coming red through his eyelids and tried, almost with desperation, to tell himself that all was right with his particular world. Everything was fine. This was the first expedition of the year to the island. The Bowdens would make three or four trips to it this year, the same as every year since 1950, when they had found it, the year before Bucky was born. It was a ridiculously small island twelve miles out into the lake, northwest of New Essex. It was too small to have a name. It merited a single dot on the charts and a warning of shoal waters. It had a hill and a beach and reasonably deep water just off the beach.

Everything was under control. The marriage was of the very best variety. Everybody was healthy. He had been a partner in the law firm ever since 1948. Their house, just outside the village of Harper, thirteen miles from New Essex, was more house than he should have purchased, but he could console himself with the constantly increasing value of the ten acres of land. They had no savings to speak of, a very few shares of pale blue-chip stocks. But his hefty insurance program gave him at feeling of security.

He raised his head and, without opening his eyes, finished off the can of beer. He told himself that there was absolutely no need to fret. No point in getting hysterical. Think of it as just another problem that could be taken care of neatly, quietly, with dispatch and efficiency.

'Hey!' Col said.

'Uh?'

'Wake up and look at me, you inert mass.'

He rolled up onto one sharp elbow and squinted at her. 'You look just fine,' he said. And she did, indeed. The pale-blue swimsuit set off her dark coloring. Her hair was black and coarse and shiny, a heritage from the remote fraction of Indian blood that had provided the inevitable name for the three boats they had owned. Her eyes were fine and dark and large. Her nose, which she despised, was high-bridged, faintly hooked. He had always liked it. Her thirty-seven years showed in the weather wrinkles at the corners of her eyes, and possibly in the veins on the backs of her hands, but not at all in the long, lithe figure, or in the round and agile legs.

'I was not fishing,' she said firmly. 'This is a serious matter. Pay attention.'

'Yes, Ma'am.'

'It started on Thursday when you came back from the office. You were physically present but spiritually among the missing. And yesterday the same. And today, more of it. Fifteen years of marriage, my remote friend, give a girl extrasensory equipment.'

'That sounds provocative. The equipment looks good on you.'

'Hush! No smart talk, Samuel. No covering up. No fencing, please, sir. I want to know. Just now you were scowling more than the sun requires. I know when something is nibbling at you.'

'In all of New Essex I am known as Subtle Sam. Nobody knows what I'm thinking. They cannot probe my Gioconda smile. I can draw and fill an inside straight without a tremor. But you have an uncanny—'

'Please,' she said in an entirely different voice, and he knew that he would have to tell her. He opened the ice chest and took out another can of beer. He opened it and offered it to her, but she shook her head. He took the can down by a third. 'All right. But understand that I'm a natural-born worrier. Everything is so good that I'm superstitious. I want to keep this very precious apple cart of ours standing on its wheels.'

'I can help you worry.'

'Or maybe laugh me out of it. I hope so. A weird thing happened when I came out of the office on Thursday. But that isn't the starting place. It starts on a certain trip overseas you might just possibly remember.'

He knew she could remember. There had been only the one trip back in 1943 when First Lieutenant Samuel B. Bowden of the Judge Advocate General's Department took a lengthy cruise on the old *Comte de Biancamano*, which was being operated by the U.S. Navy. He had embarked wearing his Pentagon pallor and had eventually ended up in New Delhi in Theater Headquarters of the C.B.I.

'I'm not fixing to forget it, lover. You were gone a good chunk of time. A good chunk out of my life. A bad chunk, I should say.'

'You haven't heard me go through the Bowden symposium of side-splitting war stories for some time, but do you happen to remember my anecdote about Melbourne? It wasn't very funny.'

'Sort of. Let me see. You got off there and you got mixed up in something and the ship went on without you because you had to be a witness, and you never caught up with that footlocker we packed with such loving care.'

'I was a key witness at a court-martial. A rape case.'

'Yes, I remember that. But I don't remember how you came to be a witness.'

'Several of us got a hotel room and I was taken drunk on Australian ale. They make it of distilled sledgehammers. It was a June night, and cold. I decided I needed the walk back to the ship. It was two in the morning. As I was getting myself thoroughly lost, I heard a whimpering in an alley. I thought it was a puppy or a kitten. But it was a girl. She was fourteen.'

He knew that the special half-drunken flavor of that night would never leave his memory. The great stone city with its wide, deserted streets, just a few lights burning.

The sound of his heels echoing coin sounds from the empty walls. He was humming 'Roll Out the Barrel.' It became nicely resonant when he was opposite the mouths of the alleys.

He decided a puppy or a kitten could be smuggled onto the ship. And then he had stopped and stared without comprehension at the pale tumbled legs, the brute rhythm of the attacker, and heard the animal whining, heard the meaty crack of his fist against her face. With comprehension had come a high-wild anger. He had wrested the soldier away from her and, as the man had scrambled up, had struck wildly and with all his strength and had hit the hard shelf of jaw. The man had grappled with him weakly, then slid down, rolled onto his back and, to Sam's astonishment, had begun to snore. He ran out and a few moments later hailed a Shore Patrol jeep.

They had held him over for the court-martial. The girl was fourteen, big for her age and very plain-looking. Her father had been sick in the night, and she had been on her way to her aunt's house to get help when the drunken soldier, Max Cady, had caught her and pulled her into the alley.

'Didn't they hang him?'

'No. But it was close. He was a twenty-five-year-old staff sergeant with seven years of service and over two hundred days of combat in the islands. He'd been pulled out with a bad case of jungle rot and jungle nerves and sent to a rest camp near Melbourne. It was his first trip into the city. He was drunk. She looked older, and she was out on the street at two in the morning.'

'But even so.'

'They gave him life at hard labor.'

He remembered how the sergeant had looked in

court. Like an animal. Sullen, vicious and dangerous. And physically powerful. Sam looked at him and knew how lucky the punch had been. Cady had looked across the court at Sam as though he would dearly enjoy killing him with his hands. Dark hair grew low on his forehead. Heavy mouth and jaw. Small brown eyes set in deep and simian sockets. Sam could tell what Cady was thinking. A nice clean noncombat lieutenant. A meddler in a pretty uniform who'd never heard a shot fired in anger. So the pretty lieutenant should have backed right out of the alley and gone on his way and left a real soldier alone.

'Sam, darling, are you trying to say that …' She had a frightened look on her face.

'Now please don't get jumpy. Don't get nervous, baby.'

'Did you see that man on Thursday? Did they let him out?'

He sighed. 'I never get a chance to finish anything. Yes. They let him out.'

He had not expected Cady to come bobbing up out of ancient history. He had merely forgotten the whole affair. Too many other impressions during those overseas years had blurred the memories of Cady. He had come home in 1945 with the rank of captain. He had got along well with his colonel, a man named Bill Stetch, and after the war he had come to New Essex at Bill's invitation and had joined the law firm.

'Tell me about it. What is he like? How in the world did he find you?'

'I don't think it's trouble. It can be handled. Anyway, when I headed for the lot on Thursday, a man I knew I'd never seen before fell in step with me. He kept grining at me in a funny way. I thought he was crazy.'

'Can we go in now? Can we? Is it time?' Bucky yelled shrilly, racing toward them.

Sam looked at his watch. 'You've been goofing off, my small, untidy friend. You could have been in five minutes ago.'

'Hey, Jamie! It's time.'

'Bucky, wait a minute,' Carol said. 'You don't go out beyond that rock. You *or* Jamie. Understand?'

'Nancy goes '*way* out.'

'And when you pass the life-saving tests she's passed, you can go '*way* out too,' Sam said. 'Don't gripe. And see if you can keep your head down.'

They watched the boys go into the water. Nancy and her friend stood up. She waved at her parents. She tucked her dark hair into her cap as she walked to the stern of the *Sweet Sioux.* Sam looked at her and felt sad and ancient as he saw how quickly her slim figure was maturing. And, as always, he thanked private gods that Nancy took after her mother. The boys took after him. Sandy-red hair, knobbly bone structure, pale-blue eyes, freckles, oversized teeth. It was evident that at maturity both boys would be like their father, incurably lean, shambling, stringy, tall men of physical indolence and ropy toughness. It would have been tragic if he had willed his only daughter such a fate.

'It was that same sergeant, wasn't it?' Carol said in a small voice,

'The same. I'd forgotten his name. Max Cady. His sentence was reviewed. He was released last September. He served thirteen years at hard labor. I wouldn't have recognized him. He's about five nine, wide and thick-set. He's more than half bald and deeply tanned, and he looks as though you couldn't hurt him with an ax. The eyes are the same and the jaw and mouth are the same, but that's all.'

'Did he threaten you?'

'Not in any explicit way. He had control of the situation. And he was enjoying himself. He kept telling me I never had the word, I never saw the picture. And he kept grinning at me. I can't remember ever seeing a more disconcerting grin. Or whiter, more artificial-looking teeth. He knew damn well he was making me uncomfortable. He followed me into the lot and I got in the wagon and started it up. Then he moved like a cat and snatched the key out and leaned on the sill, looking in at me. The car was like an oven. I sat in my own sweat. I didn't know what the hell to do. I couldn't try to take the key away from him. That's nonsense.'

'Could you have gotten out and gone after a policeman?'

'I guess so. But that didn't seem very … dignified. Like running to Teacher. So I listened. He was proud of the way he found me. When his defense officer was questioning me, it came out that I got my law degree from Penn. So Cady went to Philadelphia and got somebody to check the alumni records for him and got my home address and business address that way. He wanted to give me the word on what thirteen years of hard labor was like. He called me lieutenant. He used it in every sentence. He made it sound like a dirty word. He said that because it was June it made it sort of an anniversary for us. And he said he'd been thinking about me for fourteen years. And he said he was glad I was doing so well. He said he wouldn't have wanted to find out I had a lot of problems.'

'What … does he want to do?'

'All he said was he wanted to make sure I had the word, the big picture. I sat there sweating, and finally when I demanded my car key, he handed it to me. And he tried to give me a cigar. He had a shirt pocket full of them. He said they were good cigars. Two bits each. As I backed out he said, still grinning, 'Give my best to the wife and kids, Lieutenant.'

'It's creepy.'

Sam wondered whether he should tell her the rest of it. And then he knew he had to. She should know the rest of it so that she would not be careless – if it came to that.

He patted her hand. 'Now brace yourself, Carol-bug, This may be only in my mind. I hope so. But this is what has been chewing on me. You remember that I was late on Thursday. Cady used up a half hour. I had a lot of chance to observe him. And the more I listened, the more a little warning bell rang, louder and louder. You don't have to be a trained psychoanalyst. Somehow, when a person is different, you know it. I suppose we all run in a pack, in a sense. And there are always little clues to the rogue beast. I don't think Cady is sane.'

'My God!'

'I think you should know that about him. I may be wrong. I don't know what words the doctors would have for it. Paranoid. I wouldn't know. But he can't blame himself. I tried to tell him it was his own fault. He said if they're big enough they're old enough, and she was just another Aussie bitch. I didn't have the word. I couldn't see the picture. I think he was the type of Regular Army enlisted man who despises officers anyway. And he's come around to believing that the incident in the alley was perfectly normal. So I took thirteen years out of his life, and I should pay for it.'

'But he didn't say that?'

'No. He didn't say that. He was having a dandy time. He knew that I was squirming. What's the matter?'

Her eyes were very wide and focused. She looked beyond him. 'How long has he been in New Essex?'

'I don't know. I got the impression he'd been around a few weeks.'

'Did he have a car?'

'I don't know.'

'How was he dressed?'

'Khaki pants, not very clean. A white sports shirt with short sleeves. No hat.'

'Something happened over a week ago. Maybe it doesn't mean anything. A week ago Wednesday, I think it was. In the morning. The kids were in school. I heard Marilyn barking her fool head of and I figured she had some horribly dangerous game treed – a chipmunk or something. So I didn't pay any attention until she gave a shrill yelp. Then I went out in the yard. She was circling back through the field, tail tucked under, staring back toward the road. There was a gray car, sort of beat up, parked on the shoulder, and there was a man sitting on our stone wall, facing the house. He was well over a hundred yards away. I got the impression he was a heavy man, and he was bald, and he was smoking a cigar. I stared at him but he didn't make a move. I didn't quite know what to do. I guess Marilyn had been barking at him, but I couldn't be sure he'd thrown a stone or anything at her. If he'd just pretended to throw a stone, our courageous dog, friend of man, would have reacted the same way. And I didn't know if sitting on the wall is trespassing. The wall marks our line. So Marilyn and I went back into the house and she went under the living-room couch. The man made me sort of uneasy. You know, kind of alone out there. I told myself he was a salesman or something and he liked the view, so he stopped to sit and look at it awhile. When I looked the second time, he was still there. But the next time I looked he was gone. I don't like to think it could have been … him.'

'Neither do I. But I guess we better assume it was. Damn it, we ought to get a better dog.'

'They don't make better dogs. Marilyn isn't exactly brave, but she's sweet. Look at her.'

Marilyn, awakened from her sleep by the whooping and splashing of the kids, had gone into the water. She was a spayed red setter with a beautiful coat and good lines. She churned around after the swimming children, yipping with her spasms of joy and excitement.

'Now that I've depressed you,' he said with a heartiness he did not feel, 'I can get over onto the bright side. Even though good old Dorrity, Stetch and Bowden do corporation and estate work and handle tax matters, I do have friends in the police force. In our tidy little city of one hundred and twenty-five thousand, Sam Bowden is reasonably well known, and possibly respected. Enough so that there seems to be an idea that some day I should run for something.'

'Please don't.'

'I'm trying to say that I'm one of the boys. And the boys take care of their own. Yesterday I had lunch with Charlie Hooper, our bright young city attorney. I told him the story.'

'And I'll bet you made it sound like some kind of a joke.'

'My hands weren't trembling and I didn't look haunted, but I think I made him see that I was concerned. Charlie didn't seem to think it would be a special problem. He took down the name and description. I believe the dainty phrase he used was to have the boys 'put the roust on him.' That seems to mean that the officers of the law find so many ways on the books to lean heavily on an undesirable citizen that he departs for more comfortable areas.'

'But how could we be sure he leaves, and how would we know he wouldn't sneak back?'

'I wish you hadn't asked that question, honey. That's what I've been thinking about.'

'Why don't they put him in jail?'

'What for? My God, it would be nice if you could do that, wouldn't it? An entirely new legal system. Jail people for what they might do. New Essex toes totalitarian. Honey, listen to me. I always use the light touch, I guess, when I talk about the law business. All we moderns shy away from any hint of dedication. But I believe in the law. It's a creaking, shambling, infuriating structure. There are inequities in it. Sometimes I wonder how our system of law manages to survive. But at its base, it's an ethical structure. It is based on the inviolability of the freedom of every citizen. And it works a hell of a lot more often than it doesn't. A lot of very little people have been trying to whittle it into a new shape during these mid-years of our century, but the stubborn old monster refuses to be altered. Behind all the crowded calendars and the overworked judges and the unworkable legislation is a solid framework of equity under the law. And I like it. I live it. I like it the way a man might like an old house. It's drafty and it creaks and it's hell to heat, but the timbers are as honest as the day they were put up. So maybe it is the essence of my philosophy that this Cady thing has to be handled within the law. If the law can't protect us, then I'm dedicated to a myth, and I better wake up.'

'I guess I have to love you the way you are. Or maybe because you're the way you are, old barrister. We females are more opportunistic. I would be capable of taking that dear rifle of yours and shooting him right off our stone wall if he ever comes back.'

'You think you could. Shouldn't these two old parties try the water with the young 'uns?'

'All right. But don't start kidding Pike again. You curl him into painful knots.'

'I'm just being the jolly father of the girl friend.'

They walked toward the water. Carol looked up at him and said, 'Don't get out of touch again, Sam. Please. Let me know what goes on.'

'I'll let you know. And don't worry, I'm just superstitiously afraid because we have it so good.'

'We have it very good.'

As they stepped into the water, Nancy was clambering up over the stern of the *Sweet Sioux.* Water droplets sparkled on her bare shoulders. Her hips, so recently lanky, had begun to swell into woman-lines. She balanced herself and dived off cleanly.

Carol touched Sam's arm. 'That girl. How old was she?'

'Fourteen.' He looked into Carol's eyes. He took her wrist and held it tightly. 'Look now. Stop any of that kind of thinking. Stop it now.'

'But you've thought it too.'

'Just a moment, when you drew your little conclusion. And we'll both discard that sickening little thought right now.'

'Yes, sir.' She smiled. But the smile was not attached in

the proper and usual way. They held the look a moment longer, and then waded in. He swam out with furious energy, but he could not swim away from the sticky little tentacle of fear that had just fastened itself around his heart.

CHAPTER TWO

Sam Bowden was in his office the following Tuesday morning, going over – with a young lawyer named Johnny Karick, who had been with Dorrity, Stetch and Bowden less than a year – a trustee report from the New Essex Bank and Trust Company when Charlie Hopper phoned and said he was in the neighborhood and would it be convenient if he dropped in for a couple of minutes.

Sam finished up with Johnny quickly and sent him back to his cubicle to write a summary of the report. He called Alice on the switchboard and reception desk to send Mr. Hopper back as soon as he arrived.

Charlie came in a few minutes later and closed the office door behind him. He was a man in his early thirties, with a good-humored and ugly face, considerable energy and ambition, and a calculatedly indolent manner.

He sat down, reached for his cigarettes and said, 'Dark paneling, hushed voices, files that go all the way back to the Code of Hammurabi. And the rich smell and soft rustling of money. A working clown like me should come in on tiptoe. In between times I forget how you suave jokers make this business look almost respectable.'

'You'd die of boredom, Charlie. I spend half my time putting nice sharp points on my pencils.'

Charlie sighed. 'I'm out there in the hurly-burly of life, attending all meetings of the Common Council, and the Zoning Board and the Planning Board. Honest sweat, Samuel. Say, why don't you ever stop by Gil Brady's Courthouse Tavern any more?'

'Haven't had any courthouse business lately. And that's a sign of efficiency.'

'I know, I know. Well, I started the wheels rolling on your old buddy. He's living in a rooming house at 211 Jaekel Street, near the corner of Market. He checked in on May fifteenth. He's paid ahead until the end of June. This being only the eleventh, he had it in his mind to stay awhile. Our boys in blue check the registrations down there frequently. He drives a gray Chevy sedan about eight years old. West Virginia plates. They plucked him out of a Market Street bar yesterday afternoon. Captain Mark Dutton says he made no fuss. Very mild and patient about the whole thing.'

'Did they let him go?'

'They either have, or they're about to. They checked Kansas and found out he was released last September. They made him explain where he got money and where he got the car. Then they checked back on that. He comes from a little hill town near Charleston, West Virginia. When he was released he went back there. His brother had been working in Charleston and holding on to the home place. When Max came back, they sold it and split. He's got about three thousand bucks left and he carries it in a money belt. Charleston cleared him and Washington cleared him. His car registration and license are in order. They searched the car and his room. No gun. Nothing out of line. So they had to let him go.'

'Did he give any reason for coming here?'

'Dutton handled it the way we decided he should.

Your name wasn't brought into it. Cady said he liked the looks of the town. Dutton told me he was very cool, very plausible.'

'Did you make Dutton understand the situation?'

'I don't know. I think so. Dutton doesn't want that type drifting in any more than you do. So they'll keep an eye on him. If he spits on the sidewalk it will cost him fifty dollars. If he drives one mile an hour over the limit, it will cost him. They'll pick him up on a D-and-D when they see him coming out of a bar. He'll catch on. He'll move along. They always do.'

'Charlie, I appreciate what you've done. I really do. But I have the feeling he isn't going to scare.'

Hopper stubbed out his cigarette. 'Your nerves bad?'

'Maybe. And maybe I didn't act worried enough when we had lunch Friday. I think he's psycho.'

'If so, Dutton didn't catch it. What do you think he wants to do?'

'I don't know. I have the feeling he wants do something to hurt me the worst way he can. When you've got a wife and three kids and you live in the country, it can make you a little shaky.' He told Charlie the incident of the parked car and the man on the stone wall. The fact that Carol remembered it being a gray car made it seem more likely that it had been Cady.

'Maybe he just wants to give you a bad case of the jumps.'

Sam forced a smile. 'He's doing fine, then.'

'Maybe you can try something else, Sam. Do you know the Apex people?'

'Yes, of course. We've used them.'

'It's a national organization and in some places they're weak, but they've got some good people here, I'm thinking of one boy in particular. Sievers, his name is. He's well trained. C.I.C. background, I think. And police work too. He's rough as a cob and cold as a snake. It'll cost you, but it might be a good place to spend money. Do you know the manager over there?'

'Anderson. Yes.'

'Call him up and see if he can give you Sievers.'

'I think I'll do that.'

'Have you got Cady's address?'

'I wrote it down. Two-eleven Jaekel Street near the corner of Market.'

'Right.'

Sievers came to the office at four-thirty. He sat quietly and listened to Sam's account. He was a square-headed, gray-faced man who could have been anywhere between thirty-five and fifty. There was a bulge of softness over his belt. His hands were very large and very white. His hair was no color, and his eyes were bored slate. He made no unnecessary movements. He sat as still as a tomb and listened and made Sam feel as though he were being an alarmist.

'Mr. Anderson gave you the rates?' Sievers asked in a faraway voice.

'Yes, he did. And I promised to mail him a check right away.'

'How long do you want Cady covered?'

'I don't know. I want … an outside opinion as to whether he's planning to harm me or my family.'

'We don't read minds.'

Sam felt his face get hot. 'I realize that. And I'm not a hysterical woman, Sievers. It had occurred to me that by watching him you might get some clues as to what he has in mind. I want to know if he comes out to my house.'

'And if he does?'

'Give him as much leeway as you think safe. It would help if we could get enough evidence of his intention to convict him.'

'How do you want the reports?'

'Verbal reports will be adequate, Sievers. Can you start right away?'

Sievers shrugged. It was his first gesture of any kind. 'I've started already.'

The rain stopped just before Sam left the office that Tuesday night. The evening sun came out as he edged his way through traffic and turned onto Route 18. The route followed the lake shore for five miles through a summer resort area that was becoming more built up each year. Then it turned southwest toward the village of Harper, eight miles away, traveling through rolling farm land and past large new housing developments.

He drove into the village and around two sides of the central village square and, at the light, turned right up Milton Road Hill to his home just beyond the village limits. They had looked for a long time before they found the farmhouse in 1950, and hesitated a long time over the price. And had several estimates made on what it would cost to modernize it. But both he and Carol knew they were trapped. They had fallen in love with the old house. It sat on ten acres of farm land, all that was left of the original acreage. There were elms and oaks and a line of poplars. All the front windows overlooked a far vista of gentle hills.

The architect and the contractor had done superb jobs. The basic house was of brick painted white and was set well back from the road. The long drive was on the right-hand side of the house as you faced it, and went back to what had once been and was still called the barn, even though it was primarily to house the Ford wagon and Carol's doughty and honorable and purposeful MG. The barn was of brick too, painted white. The upstairs, which had been a hayloft, was the children's area. Marilyn, never without a whimper of alarm, could climb the wall ladder, but had to be carried down, tail furled, eyes rolling.

As Sam turned in his driveway he found himself wishing for the first time that they had close neighbors. They could see the peak of the roof of the Turner house, and some farms on the far hill slopes, but that was all. There were many houses along the road, but widely spaced. There were enough houses so that at times it seemed as though the entire population of the central school descended on the Bowden place on weekends and holidays. But no houses very close.

He drove into the barn. Marilyn came dancing, scampering and smiling in, pleading for the expected attention. Sam, as he patted her, made a bicycle count and saw that, of the three of them, only Bucky was home. It made him uneasy to think of Nancy and Jamie out on the roads. It was always a worry because of the traffic. But this was an extra worry. Yet he did not see how he could restrict them to the area.

Carol came halfway across the back yard to the barn, met him and kissed him and said, 'Did you hear from Charlie?'

'Yes. And I meant to call you, but I thought it could wait.'

'Good news?'

'Pretty good. It's a long story.' He stared at her. 'You're

looking ominously dressed up, woman. I hope there isn't a party I've forgotten about.'

'Oh, this? This was for morale. I was worried, so I got all fancied up. I generally do anyway, remember? All the happy marriage articles tell you to get dressed up for your husband every evening.'

'But not this much.'

They went in through the kitchen. He made a tall drink and took it upstairs with him to sip while he showered and changed. When he was out of the shower, Carol came and sat on the edge of her bed and listened to his account of the talk with Charlie and the employment of Sievers.

'I wish he'd done something they could arrest him for, but anyway, I'm glad about Sievers. Does he look … efficient?'

'I wouldn't know. He isn't the warmest guy anybody ever met. Charlie seems to think he's tops.'

'Charlie would know, wouldn't he?'

'Charlie would know. Stop looking so strained, baby. The wheels are in motion.'

'Isn't it going to be terribly expensive?'

'Not too bad,' he lied.

'I'm going to throw that blue shirt away sore day.'

He buttoned it, grinning at her, and said, 'When this goes, I go.'

'It's frightful!'

'I know. Where are the kids?'

'Bucky is in his room. He and Andy are designing an airplane, they say. Jamie is at the Turners', and he is invited to stay for dinner. Nancy ought to be back from the village any minute.'

'Is she with anybody?'

'She and Sandra went in on their bikes.'

He went over to the bureau and took another swallow of his drink and set the glass down. He looked at Carol. She smiled. 'I guess we can't help it, darling. The early settlers had it all the time. Indians and animals. That's what it's like. Like an animal hiding back there in the woods near the creek.'

He kissed her forehead. 'It'll be over soon.'

'It better be. I was hungry this noon, but all of a sudden I couldn't swallow. And I wanted to go down to the school and look at each one of them. But I didn't. I dug weeds in an absolute frenzy until the bus let them off in front of the house.'

He could see the drive from the bedroom window and he saw Nancy cycling toward the barn, turning to wave and yell something back over her shoulder at someone out of sight. Sandra, probably. She wore blue jean shorts and a red blouse.

'There's ole Nance,' he said, 'right on the dot.'

'She is, to use her own words, in a wild rage at Pike. There seems to be new talent at the school. Something with almost platinum hair. So now Pike is a thod.'

'Thod?'

'It was new to me too. It seems to be a combination clod and thud. The translation was given with vast impatience. Oh, *Mo*therrr!'

'I'll accept that. Pike Foster is a thod. Beyond any question. He's a phase I'll be glad to see ended. He's too meaty and muscular for a fifteen-year-old boy. And when I try to make conversation with him he blushes and stares at me and gives me the most horribly vacant laugh I've ever heard.'

'He doesn't know how to take you. That's all.'

'There's nothing opaque about me. Two-syllable words dazzle him. A true child of the television age. And of that damn school, and the damn teaching theories. And before you give me the usual smug answer, I will *not* join the PTA and try to do something about it.'

They went downstairs. Nancy was sitting on a counter in the kitchen, talking on the phone. She gave them a look of helpless boredom, covered the mouthpiece and hissed, 'I simply must study tonight.'

'Then hang up,' Sam said.

There was a sound like that of a rather underfed horse tumbling down the rear stairs. Bucky and his best friend, Andy, churned across the kitchen and out the screen door and down the steps, heading for the barn. The cylinder on the screen door sighed.

'Hello, Dad,' Sam said. 'Hello, Son. Hello, Andy. Hi, Mr. Bowden. What are you boys up to? Why, we're on our way to the barn, Dad. Fine. Run along, boys.'

Nancy, listening raptly to the voice on the other end of the line, had kicked her right sandal off. With her bare toes she was absently trying to work the latch on the cupboard under the counter. Carol had opened the wall oven and she was looking in at whatever was in there, her expression dubious and unfriendly. Carol was a good but emotional cook. She talked to the ingredients and the utensils. When something did not work out, it was not her fault. It was an act of deliberate rebellion. The darn beets decided to boil dry. The stupid chicken wouldn't relax.

Sam freshened his tall drink and took it over to the trestle table. He spread out the evening paper, but before he started to read he took a look around the kitchen. Carol had had a strong hand in the design. There was a lot of stainless steel. It was a big room. It took in the original kitchen, pantry and storeroom. A center island, with sink and burners, divided the work area from the eating area. The cupboards and cabinets were of dark pine. A big window looked out at the wooded hill behind the barn. Graduated copper pots hung against a pine wall. There was a small fieldstone fireplace near the trestle table. Sam had not been impressed at first. He had not felt comfortable in the room. Too magazinery, he had said. Too coppery quaint. But now he liked it very much, and it was the most used room in the house. The rather severe dining room, with its white woodwork and walls of Williamsburg blue, soon became reserved for state occasions. The trestle table seated five comfortably.

When Nancy hung up and retrieved her sandal, Sam said, 'Hear you have some competition, Nance.'

'What? Oh, *that*! Mother told you. She's an utterly rancid little thing. All frilly and with the cuteth little lithp and dreat big boo eyes. We all suspect she's trying out for Alice in Wonderland. The boys were positively clotted around her. A monstrous sight. Nauseous. And poor old Pike. He has absolutely no conversation, so all he could do was circle around her, bunching all his muscles. I'm in no sweat.'

'Now there is an enchantingly feminine expression.'

'Everybody says that,' she said pityingly. 'I've simply got to study. Really.'

'What comes up tomorrow, dear?' Carol asked.

'History exam.'

'Will you want any help?' Sam asked.

'Maybe on dates, later. I despise learning all those flabby old dates.'

He looked at the doorway through which she had gone.

Such a precious and precarious age. Half child and half woman. And when she was all woman, she was going to be extraordinarily lovely. And that would create its own special set of problems.

Just as he was finishing the paper, having saved Pogo for last, he heard Carol dialing. 'Hello, Liz? Carol. Is our middle child being reasonably civilized? … They are? Good. Your Mike is a perfect angel when he's here. I guess they all tend to react that way … Could I, please? Thanks, Liz … Jamie? Dear, I don't want you and Mike to goof off on the studying. You hear? … All right, dear. No elbows on the table, no audible chomping, and home by nine-thirty. Goodbye, honey.'

She hung up and turned and gave Sam a guilty glance. 'I know it's stupid. But I started worrying. And it's so easy to phone.'

'I'm glad you did.'

'If I keep this up we're all going to turn neurotic.'

'I think it's a good idea to keep a closer check on them.'

'Would you please call Bucky and send Andy home, dear?'

At nine o'clock, after seeing that Bucky was bedded down, Sam went down the hallway to his daughter's room. There was a fresh stack of records on her changer and the music was turned low. Nancy was at her desk, book and notebook open. She wore her pink terry-cloth robe. Her hair was rumpled. She gave him a look which implied that she was utterly exhausted.

'Ready for dates?'

'I guess so. I'll probably miss half of them. Here's the list, Daddy.'

'Do you even write numerals backhand?'

'It's distinctive.'

'It sure is. Don't they teach handwriting anymore?'

'It has to be legible. That's what they say.'

He went over to the bed and moved the indispensable kangaroo and sat down. She had got Sally for her first birthday, and it had shared her bed, wherever she was ever since. She no longer chewed the ears. There was very little left to chew.

'Do we do this to the background music of the gentleman with all the adenoids?'

Nancy leaned far over and turned off the player switch. 'I'm ready. Wheel and deal.'

He went through the list and she missed five. After twenty minutes she had them all, no matter how he mixed up the order. She was a bright child and highly competitive. In her own special way her mind was keenly logical, orderly, not creative. Bucky seemed to be more like Nancy. Jamie was the dreamer, the slow student, the imaginative one.

He stood up and gave her the list, hesitated, and sat down again. 'Parental department,' he said.

'I think I have a very clean conscience. At the moment, that is.'

'This is instruction, honey. Strange-men department.'

'Gosh, we've been over that a zillion times. Mom too. Don't accept rides. Don't go off in the woods alone. Don't hitchhike ever. And if anybody acts funny, run like the wind.'

'This is a little bit different, Nance. This is one specific man. I'd half decided not to tell you, but I think that would be a little stupid. This is a man who hates me.'

'Hates *you*, Daddy!'

He felt slightly annoyed. 'It is possible for somebody to hate your mild, lovable, shabby old father.'

'I didn't mean it like that. Why does he?'

'I was a witness against him a long time ago. During the war. Without my help, he wouldn't have been convicted. He's been in a military prison ever since. Now they've let him out. And he's in this area. Your mother and I believe he came out here one day a couple of weeks ago. He may do nothing at all. But we have to assume he might.'

'Why did they put him in jail?'

He looked at her for a moment, gauging her fund of knowledge.

'Rape. She was a girl your age.'

'Golly!'

'He's not as tall as I am. He's about the size of John Turner, and just as big around as John, but not soft. He's bald and quite tan, with very white, cheap-looking false teeth. He dresses poorly and smokes cigars. Can you remember that?'

'Sure.'

'Don't let any man answering that description get anywhere near you for any reason.'

'I won't. Golly, this is pretty exciting, isn't it?'

'That's one word for it.'

'Can I tell the kids?'

He hesitated. 'I don't see why not. I'm going to tell your brothers. The man's name is Cady. Max Cady.'

He stood up again. 'Don't study too long, chicken. You'll hit the exam better if you get plenty if sleep.'

'I can't wait to tell all the kids. Wow!'

He grinned at her and tousled her hair. 'Big deal, hey. Drama enters the life of Nancy Ann Bowden, subdeb. Danger stalks this scrawny lass. Tune in tomorrow for another chapter in the life of this American girl who smiles bravely while—'

'*Stop* it, now!'

'Want your door closed?'

'Hey, I nearly forgot. I saw Jake in the village. He says he's got room to pull the boat out now, and you know how he is, so I told him to go right ahead and we can work on her this weekend. Is that all right?'

'That's fine, chicken.'

When he went downstairs Jamie was back home. Carol was in the process of shooing him off to bed. Sam told him to wait a moment.

'I just told Nance about Cady,' he said.

Carol frowned and said, 'But do you think . . . Yes, I see. I think that's wise, Sam.'

'What's happening?' Jamie demanded.

'Listen very carefully, son. I'm going to tell you something and I want you to remember everything I say.'

He explained the situation to Jamie. Jamie listened intently. Sam concluded by saying, 'We'll tell this to Bucky too, but I'm not sure how much difference it will make to him. He lives in his own Martian world. So I want you to stick closer than usual to your little brother. I realize that may cramp some of your fun, but this is for real, Jamie. This isn't a television show. You'll do that?'

'Sure. Why don't they arrest him?'

'He hasn't done anything.'

'I'll bet they could arrest him. The cops have guns, see, that they've taken off dead murderers. Then they go up to the man and they shove a murder gun in his pocket and then they arrest him for carrying a gun without a license and put him in jail, see. And then they put the gun in the laboratory and they look at it through a thing and they find out it was a murder gun and so then they electrocute him, real early in the morning sometime.'

'Brother!' Carol said.

'James, my boy, the reason this is a very fine country is because that kind of thing can't happen. We don't jail innocent men. We don't jail people because we think they might do something. If that could happen, you, Jamie Bowden, might find yourself in jail sometime because somebody lied about you.'

Jamie thought it over scowlingly and then nodded. 'That Scooter Prescott would have me locked up in a minute.'

'Why?'

'Because I can do twenty-eight push-ups now, see, and when I can do fifty I'm going up to him and I'm going to punch his fat nose.'

'Does he know that?'

'Sure. I told him.'

'You better go to bed now, dear,' Carol said.

At the foot of the front stairs Jamie turned and said, 'But there's one trouble. Scooter is doing push-ups too, darn it.'

After he was gone Carol said, 'How did Nancy take it?'

'Intelligently.'

'I think it's wise to tell them.'

'I know. But it makes me feel a little ineffectual. I'm the king of this little tribe. I should be able to go put the fear of God in Cady. But I don't see how I could. Not with this office-type physique. He looks like he's got muscles they haven't named yet.'

'Is that Marilyn?'

He went out into the kitchen and let her in. She waggled and beamed at him and flounced over to her dish, stared with shock and disbelief at its emptiness, then turned and looked up at him.

'No dice, girl. You're on a diet, remember?'

She slooped disconsolately at her water dish, trudged over to her corner, turned around three times and sighed as she collapsed onto her side. Sam sat on his heels beside her and prodded her stomach gently with his finger.

'Got to get your girlish figure back, Marilyn. Got to get rid of that flab.'

She rolled an eye at him and the long red brush of tail flapped twice. She yawned, with a little yowl at the end of the yawn, exposing the long white ivory fangs.

He stood up. 'A great savage beast. Dismayed by kittens. Bedeviled by vicious squirrels. Every day is a hard day, Marilyn, for a four-year-old devout coward, isn't it?'

The tail flapped dreamily and she closed her eyes. He wandered back into the living room, yawned. Carol looked at him and yawned.

'I caught it from Marilyn; you caught it from me.'

'So I'm taking it to bed.'

'Make sure Nance has hit the sack,' he said. 'I'll be right along.'

He turned off the lights, started to lock the front door and then opened it again and went out into the front yard, strolled down toward the road. Rain had washed the air clean, and it had the smell of June and the promise of summer. The stars looked small and high and newly polished. He heard the dwindling snarl of a truck on Route 18 and, after it died, the remote song of a dog on a far-off farm across the valley. A mosquito whined in his ear and he waved it away.

The night was dark and the sky was high, and the world was a very large place. And a man was almost excessively small, puny and vulnerable. His brood was abed.

Cady lived somewhere in this night, breathing the darkness.

He slapped at the mosquito and walked back across the damp grass to the house, locked up, and went up to bed.

CHAPTER THREE

Sievers reported to Sam in his office at ten on Thursday morning. He sat in his very still way and did not change expression as he spoke in his flat, bored voice.

'I picked him up at six o'clock coming out of the rooming house. He walked to Nicholson's bar three blocks down Market Street. He came out alone at seven-thirty and walked back and got his car and drove to Nicholson's and double-parked and blew the horn and a woman came out and got in the car with him. A fat blonde with a loud laugh. He drove back to the rooming house and put the car in the back where he keeps it and they went in together and came back out about forty minutes later. They got in the car and I followed them. He started turning too many corners. I couldn't tell if he'd made me or he was being cute or maybe they were just looking for a place to eat. I had to hang 'way back. Finally they headed out of town on Route 18. He turned onto a secondary road. No traffic. He bluffed me by slowing 'way down after he was around a bend. So I had to pass. When I was out of sight I turned off and cut the lights, but he didn't come along. So that means he was cute. I came back fast, but he had too many choices of turns. So I went back to Nicholson's. He goes there a lot, I found out. They know him only as Max. The woman is one of those Market Street characters. Bessie McGowan. Not quite a prostitute, but so close the difference doesn't show. He brought her back at three in the morning to the rooming house. He was okay, but he nearly had to carry her in. I knocked off and went back at ten-thirty yesterday morning. He came out at a quarter of twelve, drove to a delicatessen and took a sack of food back to the room. At five o'clock he drove her to one of those beat-up apartment hotels on Jefferson Avenue and went in with her. They came out at seven and she'd changed outfits. They went back to Nicholson's. He came out alone at nine and started walking. He headed down toward the lake front. He was having fun. He's awake every minute. He's cute and he's good. He can see in all directions at once. And he can move. I lost him. I thought I'd lost him. Then he lit his damn cigar right next to me. I nearly jumped out of my shoes. He gave me a good look and grinned and said, 'Nice night for it,' and walked back to Nicholson's. He took her to dinner at a steak house five miles out of town by the lake. They got back to the rooming house at three again. So I guess they're still there. I goofed and I've got no apologies. What do you want next?'

'Should the agency put a different man on him?'

'I'm the best, Mr. Bowden. I'm not trying to kid you. He'd make the next one just as quick, or quicker.'

'I don't quite understand, Does it make any special difference that he saw you and can recognize you? Can't you keep an eye on him anyway?'

'I could set up a team to do it, but even then it might not work. Three men and three cars, and a second shift so you could cover him around the clock. But there's too many ways he can give us the slip. Go in a movie and go out any exit. Go in a department store and go upstairs and come down another way and go out another door.

Go out through the kitchen of any joint. Go play games in a hotel. There's too many ways.'

'What do you suggest, Sievers?'

'Drop it. You're wasting your money. He expected to be covered. So he was looking for it. He'll keep on looking for it. And any time be wants to shake loose, he'll figure out a way. This one is cool and smart.'

'You aren't much help. You don't seem to understand that this man wants to harm me. That's why he came here. He may try to get at me through my family. What would you do?'

The slate eyes seemed to change color, turn lighter. 'Change his mind.'

'How?'

'Don't quote me. I'd make some contacts. Bounce him into the hospital a couple of times, he gets the point. Work him over with some bicycle chain.'

'But . . . maybe he isn't planning anything.'

'This way you're sure.'

'I'm sorry, Sievers. Maybe it's a weakness in me, but I don't think so. I can't operate outside the law. The law is my business. I believe in due process.'

Sievers stood up. 'It's your money. A type like that is an animal. So you fight like an animal. Anyway, I would. If you change your mind, we can have a private talk. This wouldn't be through the agency. You'll waste money keeping me on his tail.'

He paused at the door and looked back, his hands on the knob. 'You have to figure one angle on this. You've alerted the law. If he does anything, he sure as hell is going to be picked up. But then again, maybe he doesn't give a damn.'

'What would that team cost?'

'Somewhere around two thousand a week.'

After Sievers was gone Sam tried to lose himself in his work, but his attention kept wandering back to Cady. As he drove home Thursday night, he decided there would be no point in telling Carol that Sievers was no longer on the job. It would be difficult to explain and would alarm her unnecessarily.

Carol called him at three o'clock on Friday afternoon. When he heard her tone of voice his hand clamped tightly on the phone. She was nearly incoherent.

'Carol, are the kids all right?'

'Yes, yes. They're all right. It's that . . . that fool dog.' Her voice broke. 'Could you come home? Please.'

On his way out he stopped in Bill Stetch's office and told him there was trouble at home. The dog had probably been run over, and he was leaving for the day.

He made good time on the way home. It was a gray day. Carol came walking quickly out to the barn, the kids trailing after her. Carol looked haggard and gray. Nancy was pasty white, her eyes swollen and red. Jamie held a trembling mouth clamped tightly shut. Bucky stumbled along, fists in his eyes, bellowing in such a hoarse way that Sam knew he had been crying for a long time.

Carol turned around, her voice sharp, and said, 'Nancy, you take the boys back in the house, please.'

'But I want to—'

'Please!' Carol seldom spoke so harshly to them.

They went back toward the house. Bucky was still roaring. Carol turned back to him and her eyes filled with tears. 'God deliver me from another forty minutes like I had today.'

'What happened? Run over? Is she dead?'

'She's dead. But she wasn't run over. Dr. Lowney came right out. He was perfectly wonderful. We couldn't get her in the MG to take her in. The timing was absolutely superb. I heard the school bus stop and then pull away, and then I heard Nancy screaming. I came running out like I was shot out of a gun. I found out later that when the bus was coming to a stop Jamie looked out the window and saw Marilyn in the front yard, gobbling something down. She came prancing over to meet the kids as she always does, and then she started to whine and run in circles and bite herself in the side. Then she went into a kind of convulsion. That's what started Nancy screaming.' The tears ran down Carol's face. 'When I got there the dog was in agony. I've never seen anything so pitiful or frightening. And all three kids watching. I tried to get near her, but she snapped at me so viciously I didn't dare touch her. I told the kids not to touch her and I ran in and phoned Dr. Lowney. I looked out the window and she was still having those spasms and the kids weren't too close, so I phoned you. She was rolling and writhing and making the most awful screaming noise I ever heard a dog make. I didn't want the kids to watch, but I couldn't get them away. Then she began to run down, like a clock or a machine or something. Dr. Lowney arrived just before the end. She died about a minute later. So he took her in with him. That was about twenty minutes ago.'

'He said she was poisoned?'

'He said it looked like it.'

'Damn it to hell!' His eyes were stinging.

'It would have been bad enough just to see it, but to have the kids see it too! This is going to be a cheery household this weekend.'

'Can you handle the kids for a little while?'

'Where are you going? Oh, down to the vet's?'

'Yes.'

'Please don't be long.'

Dr. Lowney was a big placid man with white hair, bright-blue eyes and an easygoing manner. When Sam went into the waiting room Mrs. Lowney, behind the desk, bobbed her head at him and went into the back and came out immediately and said, 'The doctor would like you to go right on back, Mr. Bowden. All the way back.'

A waiting woman with a toy black poodle on her lap gave Sam a concentrated glare. He walked back. Lowney stood at a work bench. Marilyn was on a stained wooden table in the middle of the small room. The life had gone out of her coat. She lay like a dull red rag, one white slit of eye showing.

Lowney turned from the bench. There was no greeting, no affability. 'I haven't got the best lab resources in the world, Sam, but I'm pretty sure it was strychnine, and a walloping big dose of it. It was administered in raw meat. Probably just cut a slit in a piece of meat and stuffed the crystals in.'

One of her ears was folded back. Sam unfolded it. 'It makes me feel so mad I feel sick.'

Lowney stood on the other side of the table and they both looked down at the dead dog. 'I don't get much of this, thank God. I'm in this business purely and simply because I've been nuts about animals ever since I could crawl. I have the belief that poisoning an animal is a more vicious and callous thing than murdering a human. They can't understand. It's a dirty shame the kids saw it.'

'Maybe they were meant to see it.'

'What do you mean by that?'

'I don't know. I don't know what I mean.'

'Sam, I wish you'd let me talk you into taking her to obedience school last year.'

'It seemed like too much trouble somehow.'

'Then she'd never have touched that meat.'

'We had her on a diet. She was an incorrigible beggar. And scared of her own shadow. But she was one hell of a wonderful dog. She had personality. Damn it all.'

'There isn't much you can do about it, you know. Even if you could prove who did it, it's just a fine, and not much of one at that. I don't suppose you want me to dispose of her.'

'No. I suppose I could take her back.'

'Why don't you go back and decide where you want to bury her and get a big enough hole dug, and I'll drop her by after I close up here at five. I'll wrap her in something. No need for the kids to have to look at her again. She isn't so pretty.'

'I don't want to put you to any trouble.'

'Trouble, hell. You go dig the hole.'

When Sam walked into the house Carol had managed to get Bucky quieted down. He was in the living room staring woodenly at television. His face was bloated and, at metronomic intervals, a strangled sob shook him like a massive hiccup. Carol was in the kitchen. He noted with instant approval that Marilyn's dishes and rug had been put away out of sight.

'Where's Nance and Jamie?'

'In their rooms. Did Dr. Lowney know what…'

'Strychnine.'

They were speaking in hushed voices. She turned into his ams and he held her. She spoke against the side of his throat, 'I keep telling myself it was just a fool dog. But ...'

'I know.'

She turned back toward the sink. 'Who would do such a horrible thing, Sam?'

'It's hard to say. Somebody with a twisted mind.'

'But it isn't as if she was ranging around killing chickens or digging up flower beds. She never went off the place unless she was with the kids.'

'Some people just don't like dogs.'

She turned around, wiping her hands on a dish towel, her expression grim and intent. 'You're never home when the school bus comes, Sam. Marilyn knew the sound it makes when it comes up the hill. And wherever she was, she'd start heading out for the end of the drive and be there waiting when it stopped. If somebody followed the bus in a car they'd know about that. And then the next time they could go ahead of the bus and throw that poisoned stuff out where she'd be sure to find it when she came to meet the bus.'

'It could have been just a coincidence.'

'I think you know better than that. I think you feel the same way I do. I'm not being hysterical. There're dogs all along Milton Road, I've been trying to think of who doesn't have one, and the only ones are the Willeseys. And they're over a mile from here and they've got all those cats and they wouldn't poison a dog anyway. And we've lived here seven years now, and I've never heard of such a thing happening. So, the first time it happens, why was it *our* dog?'

'Now, Carol ...'

'Don't you "now, Carol" me. We're both thinking the same thing and you know it. Where was that wonderfully efficient private eye?'

Sam sighed. 'All right. He's not on the job any more.'

'When did he stop?'

'Wednesday night.'

'And just why did he stop?'

He explained Sievers' reasons to her. She listened intently, expressionlessly, mechanically continuing to dry her hands on the towel.

'And just when did you know all this?'

'Yesterday morning.'

'And you didn't say a word last night. I was to go on thinking everything was just dandy. You had it all fixed. I'm not a child and I'm not a fool and I resent being … overprotected.'

'I should have told you. I'm sorry.'

'So now this Cady can roam around at will and poison our dog and work his way up to the children. Which do you think he'll start on first? The oldest or the youngest?'

'Carol, honey. Please.'

'I'm a hysterical woman? You are so damn right. I am a hysterical woman.'

'We haven't any proof it was Cady.'

She threw a towel into the sink. 'Listen to me. *I* have proof it was Cady. I've got that proof. It's not the kind of proof you would like. No evidence. No testimony. Nothing legalistic. I just *know.* What kind of a man are you? This is your *family.* Marilyn was part of your *family.* Are you going to look up all the precedents and prepare a brief?'

'You don't know how—'

'I don't know anything. This is happening because of something you did a long time ago.'

'Something I had to do.'

'I'm not saying you shouldn't have. You tell me the man hates you. You don't think he's sane. So *do* something about him!'

She had taken a step closer to him, glaring at him quite fiercely. And then her face crumpled and she was in his arms again, shivering this time. He held her and then he took her over to the bench by the trestle table and sat beside her, holding her hand.

She tried to smile and said, 'I despise sniveling women.'

'You have the best reason in the world to be upset, honey. I know how you feel. And I know you've got cause for complaint. I provide food, clothing and shelter. Very civilized. It would be a hell of a lot easier to handle Cady during more primitive times, or in a more primitive part of the world. I am a member of a social complex. He is the outsider. I would rally my gang and we would kill him. I would very much like to kill him. I might even be able to manage it. You are reacting on a primitive level. That is actually what your instinct tells you I should do. But your logic will tell you how impossible that is. I would be sent to prison.'

'I . . . I know.'

'You want me to be effectual and decisive. That is precisely what I want to be. I don't think I can frighten him away. I can't kill him. The police are being less help than I thought they would be. There are two things I can think of. I can see Captain Dutton on Monday and see if he'll cooperate the way Charlie promised he would. And if that doesn't seem to work out, then we'll move out of his range.'

'How?'

'School will be over next week.'

'Wednesday is the last day.'

'You can take off with the kids and find a place to stay and phone me at the office when you get located.'

'But you shouldn't . . .'

'We can close the house and I'll take a hotel room in town. I'll be careful. This thing can't last forever.'

'But between now and then . . .'

'I'm not certain of anything. But I can make a guess about how his mind works. He isn't going to rush. He's going to give us some time to think this over.'

'Can we be more careful anyway?'

'I'll use the MG next week. You can drive the kids in in the wagon and pick them up after school. And I'll give orders they're to stay on the place. And tomorrow you get some target practice with the Woodsman.'

She linked her fingers in his. 'I'm sorry I blew up. I shouldn't have. I know you'll do everything you can, Sam.'

'I've got to dig a grave for Marilyn. Doc Lowney is going to leave her off here. Where do you think?'

'How about that slope behind the barn near the aspens? That's where they buried the bird that time.'

'I'll go change.'

He put on faded, paint-spattered dungarees and his old blue shirt. He sensed that Carol was right. Instinct had told her Cady had poisoned the dog. He found it curious he should be willing to accept that with so little proof. It was contrary to his training, to all his instincts.

He looked in on Jamie in his room. The plastic radio, its red case mended with tar tape, was turned on. Jamie sat on the bed leafing through one of his dog-eared gun catalogues. He looked up at his father and said, 'It was really poison, wasn't it?'

'Yes, it was.'

'And that man that hates us did it?'

'We don't know who did it, son.'

The young eyes were pale and blue and hard. He held the catalogue out. 'You see that thing? It's a blunderbuss. With a brass barrel. Mike and me are going to get some f.f.g. powder and get this blunderbuss and I'm going to put a double load in it and I'm going to fill it all the way up with thirty old rusty nails and stuff and I'm going to hit that old Cady right in the gut. Pow!' Tears stood in his eyes.

'Mike knows about it?'

'I called him up while you were gone. He cried too but he was pretending he wasn't. He wanted to come over but I told him I didn't want him to.'

'Want to help me pick a spot for the grave?'

'Okay.'

They got a spade from the barn. A cairn of pebbles held upright the tiny cross that marked the grave of Elvis, the deceased parakeet. Elvis had had the freedom of the house and was up to two words when Bucky, four years old then, had stepped on him. Bucky's feeling of guilt and horror had lasted for so long they had begun to worry about him.

Sam got the hole well started and then let Jamie take his turn. The boy worked with dogged violence, grim-faced. As Sam stood watching, Nancy came up to him, walking slowly.

'This is a good place,' she said, 'Did you bring her back?'

'Doc Lowney is going to bring her.'

'I saw you from my window. Damn it all, anyway.'

'Easy, girl.'

'Mother thinks that man did it.'

'I know she does. But there's no proof.'

Jamie stopped digging. 'I could dig a bigger hole. I could dig a hole for him and drop him down in it with snakes and things, and fill it with rocks and stomp it all down on him.'

Sam could see the boy was winded. 'I'll take a turn now. Let's have the shovel.'

They stood and watched him finish it. Lowney arrived. He had the dog wrapped in a tattered old khaki blanket. Sam lifted her out of the car and carried her to the hole. She was extremely heavy. He covered her quickly and shaped the mound with the shovel. Dr. Lowney refused the offer of a drink and drove on back to town.

Dinner was a cheerless affair. During dinner Sam outlined the new rules. He had half expected objections. But the kids accepted them without comment.

After the children were all in bed, Sam and Carol sat in the living room.

'It's so hard on them,' Carol said. 'Bucky most of all. He was two when we got her, and she was sort of his dog.'

'I'll do a little slave-driving tomorrow. Make them all work on the boat. It'll take their minds off it.'

'And some target practice?'

'You sound eager. You were pretty reluctant the last time.'

'Because there didn't seem to be much point in it.'

They read for a while. He got up restlessly and looked out at the night. There was a distant grumble of June thunder. It sounded as though it came from the north, out over the lake. Marilyn had always had a standard reaction to thunder. The head would go up and tilt. Then the ears would go back. She would stand up and give a vastly artificial yawn, lick her chops, eye them in a side-long way and saunter in the general direction of the couch. With one more apologetic glance she would crawl under the couch. Once when a loud clap of thunder had come without previous warnings from the distance, she had shot across the room and miscalculated the clearance and banged her forehead mightily on the bottom edge. She had rebounded, staggered, recovered, and scrambled under, and everybody had laughed except Bucky.

'It was like a charmed circle,' Carol said.

He turned and looked at her. 'I think I know what you mean.'

'The untouchables. And now something has come in out of the darkness and struck one of us down. The charm isn't working any more.'

'The business of living is a very precarious occupation.'

'Don't be philosophical with me. Let me have my ridiculous little superstitions. We had a nice little fool's paradise.'

'And will have again.'

'It won't be the same.'

'You've had a grim day.'

She stood up and stretched. 'And I'm going to put an end to it right now. This was a real whistler of a day. A doozy.' The thunder sounded again, closer. 'Let's lock up the joint,' she said.

'I'll do it. You run along. I'll be right up.'

After she had gone up he stood in the back of the house and watched the northwest sky. There were pink flashes below the horizon line. It would have been easier for all of them, he thought, if Marilyn had been a valiant, brave and noble animal. But she had been such a hapless creature, full of alarms and forebodings, yelping at the mere threat of pain, constantly in a state of apology. It was as though all her fears had come true, as though she had always known of the special agony awaiting her.

CHAPTER FOUR

All five Bowdens had breakfast, for once, at the same time. There was discussion of the violence of the storm that had struck in the night. Jamie and Bucky had not heard it at all. Nancy said it had awakened her and she had put her robe on and sat by her window and watched it. Neither Sam nor Carol mentioned that Carol, wakened by the storm and timid of lightning, had slid over into Sam's bed, cuddling in fragrant closeness to still her fears. Marilyn was not mentioned. But Bucky had shadowy hollows under his eyes.

'Schedule,' Sam said. 'Attention, all Bowdens. Nancy will help her mother swamp out the kitchen and make the beds while you boys help me find the stuff for the boat and load it in the wagon. Then we shall have a spot of target practice. You are in charge of hanging up the cans, Jamie. Then we go work on the boat.'

The range was part way up the gentle hill behind the house. The backstop was a clay bank. Jamie got a half dozen empty cans from the rubbish and tied cord on them and hung them from a red maple limb in front of the clay bank. They used up a box and a half of longs in the .22 automatic. Sam and Nancy were the best shots. Jamie, as usual, became infuriated with himself when Nancy outshot him. Carol did better than she had done in the past. She did not try to give up her turn. She listened with care to the hints Sam give her. She did not flinch as badly. Sam, standing behind her and off to one side, saw the set of her jaw and her frown of concentration. The kids were much quieter than usual. This had been a game they had played often. Today it was more than a game. There was a new flavor to it, sensed by all of them.

On Bucky's final turn he hit three of the riddled cans at sixty feet with an eight-shot clip. He flushed red with pride at the congratulations.

'Shall I take the cans down?' Jamie asked.

'Leave them up,' Sam said. 'Maybe we'll get a little more practice in tomorrow afternoon. If we finish the boat.'

'How about their homework?'

'Tonight and tomorrow night,' Sam said.

'I was going to the drive-in tonight,' Nancy said in a complaining tone.

'Forgotten the new rules already?' Sam asked.

'No, but gosh, Dad, I'd already said yes.'

'And just who has a car to take you to the drive-in?'

'Well, his name is Tommy Kent and he's a senior and he's eighteen so he can drive at night, and it's a double date, sort of, and Sandra is going with Bobby.'

'Is that the family that has the furniture store?' Carol asked.

'Yes, and it would be all right, honestly. They'll pick me up right here and we'll come right back after the movie. It's with John Wayne. I was going to ask about it Friday, but . . . on account of Marilyn I forgot. Can't I go, please? Just this time?'

Sam looked at Carol and saw the almost imperceptible nod. 'All right. But just this once. And how did you do on the history?'

'Pretty good, I think.'

'You kids run along and get ready. We're going to the boat yard right now.'

They ran down the hill. Sam and Carol followed more slowly. Sam said, 'You crossed me up.'

'I know. But I think this will be all right. And you would have no possible idea of how much I've heard about Tommy Kent, Tommy Kent, Tommy Kent. Before and during the Pike Foster era. He's a school figure. A big athlete. It's quite a coup for a junior-high girl to get a date with him.'

'I suppose. But I wish she'd get tired of the muscle set.'

'This one isn't as dull as poor Pike. Tommy waited on me at the store one Saturday. When I was buying that lamp for the study last August. He's quite a poised young man.'

'He's probably too poised, damn it. Too sophisticated for Nance. She's only fourteen. I don't want her hot-rodding around in the night, going to those drive-ins. What do they call them? Passion pits. And they make jokes about never seeing the movie.'

'Now stop being the traditional father, darling. If we haven't given Nance a good set of moral standards by now, it's much too late to start. She's nearly fifteen. Sandra will be along. And no two determined young men are going to separate them. She will very probably be kissed.'

'It makes me writhe to think of it.'

'Be brave, darling. She'll be safe and it will be better than having her gloom round. Pike's desertion really hurt her morale. And this date built it back up again.'

'The damn car probably has no brakes, weak lights, and bald-headed tires.'

'It happens to be a brand-new Plymouth two-door sedan.'

'I forgot the mark-up on furniture. What's with Jamie?'

Jamie had let the other two go ahead. He stood by Marilyn's fresh grave, waiting for them. When they came up to him he said fiercely, 'We're going to have a big marble monument. With dates and her name.'

'We'll have to have something, Son,' Sam said. 'But a big marble marker would be pretentious, wouldn't it?'

'What do you mean?'

'It ought to be simpler. I'll bet if you and Mike scouted the creek bed, you could find a good stone with a flat side on it. Then I think we could chisel her name in it.'

When Jamie looked dubious, Carol said, 'I think that would look very nice, dear.'

Jamie sighed. 'Okay. We'll look. Ever since I got up I keep feeling like I see her around. Sort of over to the side. Like if I turned my head quick enough I could see her.'

Carol hugged him against her side. 'I know, dear. We all feel the same way.'

Jamie looked at his father from the circle of his mother's arm. 'We could find where he eats and sneak in the kitchen and put something in his food and then when he eats it we could be looking through those round windows they have in the doors of the kitchens in restaurants and he'd be rolling around knocking tables over and everybody screaming until he's all quiet and dead.'

'Those pants are too good for boat work,' Carol said. She gave him a little push. 'You run in the house and put on the rattiest pair of jeans you can find in your closet.'

'The ones you said were too far gone to patch?'

'Those will be perfect.'

Jamie ran off. Carol said, 'I wonder if it's healthy, the

way his imagination works. Some of the things he comes out with are shocking.'

'At eleven civilization is still a thin coating. Underneath is all savage.'

'Sir, you are speaking of the children I love.'

'They run in packs, pick on the weak ones and the different ones, gloat on thoughts of dreadful torture. It's part of survival, darling. In wartime, in the big cities, they survive, when the ones a little older, softened up a little more by the moralities, perish.'

'Sometimes you get ridiculously objective. I'm thinking of Jamie. He has such violent ideas.'

'Speaking of violent ideas, can you manage to keep the automatic handy without being obvious about it?'

'I think so. My big straw bag.'

'It won't make you feel too melodramatic?'

'I am not going to let you make me feel self-conscious about it. It's a gun. It shoots. And I am not squeamish a bit. You've showed me how the safety works. I'm going to keep one shell in the chamber. My brood is threatened, Samuel, and I'm turning just as primitive as Jamie. While I was shooting up there I kept wondering if I could point it at a human being and pull the trigger and keep the sights lined up and not flinch. And I thought about Marilyn and I know I can.'

'You impress me.'

The New Essex Yacht Club is four miles east of the city. It has an ample yacht basin, dock space, its own breakwater, a long club building, with terraces, bars and ballroom. The motor-cruiser owners call the devout sailors the Magellan Set. The sailors call the cruiser owners the Stinkpot Group. Large yachts stop at New Essex because the facilities are good. In the summer there are visitors from Miami and Fort Lauderdale. In the winter several of the local owners of the big cruisers head south.

After Sam and Carol graduated from the *Sweet Sioux II*—a converted lifeboat from an obsolete lake ferry—to the *Sweet Sioux III*—a cranky twenty-six feet of day cruiser about sixteen years old, with convertible navy top—they joined the New Essex Yacht Club. The dues were high, and the social schedule was intensive. The *Sweet Sioux*, no matter how fresh her current paint and varnish job, never looked at ease tied up in the middle of all that teak, brass, chrome and mahogany. She had a beamy and disreputable look, like a dressed-up washer-woman at the opera.

She seemed actively to resent her new environment. On each departure she tried to swing and bash one of the grand craft tied up near her. She had a single screw and a sixty-five horse power marine engine of a make few people had ever heard of. The engine was stolid, reliable and unaccountably quiet. It could push the *Sweet Sioux* along at a waddling ten knots. But at the New Essex Yacht Club the engine also revolted. Twice it quit in the middle of the basin as they were headed in. And twice they had to accept a tow. After that Sam kept a five-horse outboard motor wrapped in a tarp stowed forward.

The club was expensive and too many of the members were excessively stuffy. And it was a long way from Harper. When it came time to pay dues for the second year, Sam and Carol talked it over and were each pleased and surprised to find how willingly the other person would give up the club.

They joined the Harper Boat Club. It was ten miles

closer, on the lake shore between New Essex and Harper, at the end of a road that turned off Route 18. The club building could more accurately be called a shack. The boat basin was small and crowded. Jake Barnes's boat yard was next door to the club. It was a cluttered, informal enterprise. He sold boats, gas, oil, gear, fishing tackle and cold beer. He was a fat, sleepy man who had inherited the business when his father died. He was a good but indolent craftsman. He had rickety ways on which he could haul anything up to forty feet out of the water. He had a good touch with marine engines and outboards and, when pressed, could do major hull repairs. His yard was an incredible clutter of timbers, corroding hardware, empty oil cans, hulls too far gone for repair, rotting lines and sagging roofs over his covered storage area.

Most members of the Harper Boat Club were ardent do-it-yourself addicts. This seemed to please Jake. He charged a nominal fee for hauling the boats out. He seemed happiest when he could stand in dirty tee shirt and soiled duck pants drinking his own beer and watching the clientele work on their boats. The children of the members of the neighboring club adored Jake. He told them all kinds of monstrous lies of his adventures.

The *Sweet Sioux* took kindly to the change. Here she looked almost modern. After the opera the washerwoman had returned to the neighborhood saloon and was content. The marine engine no longer conked out. And Sam and Carol had a lot more fun at club affairs. The group was younger.

Sam parked the station wagon in the rear of Jake's boat yard and checked off the things they had brought. Sandpaper, calking material and calking compound, antifouling marine hull paint, deck paint and varnish.

Jake, with a can of beer in his large dirty hand, ambled over to meet them as they came around the side of the main shed.

'Hi, Sam. Howya, Mizz Bowden. Hello, kids.'

'Did you get her out?' Nancy asked.

'Sure did. Right down there on the last cradle. She needs some work, all right. Looked her over yesterday. Want to show you something, Sam.'

They walked down to the *Sweet Sioux*. Out of the water she looked twice as big and half again as ugly.

Jake finished his beer and threw the can aside, took out a pocket knife, opened the small blade and went around to the transom. As Sam watched, he dug the blade into the rear of the keel just forward of the prop. The blade went in with alarming ease. Jake straightened up and gave Sam a significant look.

'Rotten?'

'It's rotted some. The last two, three feet of the keel.'

'Is that dangerous?'

'I'd say if a fellow let it go too long it might give him some trouble after a while.'

'Should I do something right away?'

'Now, I wouldn't say right away. Busy as I am this time of year, it would be some time before I could get to her. Then I'd say cut it back to about here. Cut this whole section right out. Then cut a good choice piece to fit and bolt it up right here, and then put some plate braces on both sides along here and bolt them all the way through. I checked the rest of her over and she's still sound.'

'When should I do it, Jake?'

'I'd say after I pull her out in October is time enough. Then you'll have the use of her all summer. Now, come around here and I'll show you where the bad leak is. Right here. See. The planking is a little sprung and it opened up this here crack. Water run out of her real good right at that place.'

'Isn't that a little wide to calk?'

Jake reached under the boat and picked up a thin piece of wood off the crossbar of the cradle. 'I whittled this piece out and it seems to fit okay. I was going to soak it good with waterproof glue and pound it in there, but I didn't get around to it. I guess you could handle that okay. I'll show you where the glue pot is, Sam. Now, I want to see you kids turn out some work today. No runnin' off like the last time, Bucky. You sand good and you'll raise yourself a crop of muscle. You bring old Marilyn along to help you? … What's the matter? I say something wrong?'

'Let's go get that glue,' Sam said. On the way up to the shed he told Jake about the dog.

Jake spat accurately at an empty oil drum. 'Take a special mean kind of son of a bitch to poison a dog.'

'I know.'

'There was a fella here before your time, when my daddy was alive. Most folks say fish got no feelings. Cold blood and all. But he used to clean his fish here, and he'd take them alive out of the bait well and scale 'em and fillet 'em still wiggling. Seemed to get a kick out of it. We run him off the place finally. Lost a bait customer. Some people got a mean streak all right. It's surely hell on those kids. That wasn't much of a dog for a fight, but she sure liked friends. Here's the glue. Let me get that top for you. Use this here rubber mallet and don't try to get it in too fast. Little taps, and keep it even. Don Langly's setter bitch had another litter couple of weeks ago. She jumped the fence again. Don thinks it was a chow dog got to her this time, but those pups are sure cute. He's trying to find homes for them for when they're weaned.'

'Thanks, Jake. But maybe later on.'

'Sometimes it's good to get another one right away. I'd say a little more glue. Slop it on good. You can wipe of what squeezes out.'

After the family had watched him tap the whittled wedge into place, Sam apportioned the work. They all began to work, using the sanding blocks. The sun was hot and it was tiring work. After a half hour Sam took off his shirt and hung it on a sawhorse. The slight breeze of the lake cooled the perspiration on his lean back. Bucky was unexpectedly solemn and diligent.

When Gil Burman came by and stopped, Sam used it as an excuse to call a break. Jamie and Bucky raced off with a dollar to buy two beers and three Cokes from Jake.

'You got this crew organized,' Gil said. Gil was a forty-year-old vice-president of the New Essex Bank and Trust Company. He had moved out to Harper a year ago. He was a big man, prematurely gray. His wife was a vivacious and rattle-brained redhead. Sam and Carol liked and enjoyed Gil and Betty.

'He's a whip snapper,' Carol said.

'I lost my helpers on account of the pram race this afternoon. They're getting organized.'

'Does the *Jungle Queen* need work?'

'Does she ever not need it? Dry rot in the dashboard this time. Damn old clunker. Why we keep her, I'll never know. Carol, did Betty get in touch with you yet about next Friday?'

'No, not yet.'

'A big old Burman soiree, kids. Cindered steaks in the back yard. An extensive clobbering on Martinis. Drunken conversation and family battles afterward. We have to do it for a lot of sordid types, and so we need some of our friends around to improve the situation.'

Carol glanced at Sam and then said to Gil, 'We'd love to come. But there may be a hitch. I might have to be out of town. I could let Betty know later in the week?'

'Right up until kickoff. It's a big party.'

The boys came back with the Cokes and beer. Sam went off to one side to talk business with Gil. The bank acted as trustee on many of the estates represented by Dorrity, Stetch and Bowden. As they talked, Sam looked idly at his family. Carol was getting them back to work. Nancy wore very short red shorts, old and faded, and a yellow linen halter. Her legs were long and brown and slim, beautifully shaped. She worked the sanding block with both hands, turning lithely at the waist. The smooth young muscles bunched and lengthened under the sheen and texture of her back.

After Gil left he worked again, steadily, and by one o'clock Carol announced it was time for a lunch break. They would run home and eat and come back. It was then that Nancy announced, quite demurely, that she had told Tommy Kent what they'd be doing and he had said he might stop around and help, so, if it was all right, she would stay and keep working and they could bring her back a sandwich, please.

Sam drove Carol and the boys home. Mike Turner was sitting on the front porch, waiting for Jamie. Carol made hefty sandwiches and a giant pitcher of iced tea. As she was wrapping Nancy's sandwich, Carol said, 'You itching to get back to work?'

'I'd like to get that hull painted before dark.'

'I'm going to make Bucky take a nap. He's completely pooped. He'll yelp at the idea, but he'll cork off in about ten seconds. You go on ahead and bring the boys down in an hour or so.'

He took the MG and drove back to the boat yard. He walked around the shed, carrying the sandwich and a small thermos of iced tea. Nancy was sitting on her haunches, sanding the undercurve of the hull, a difficult place to get at. She smiled up at him.

'No dreamboat yet?'

'Not yet, Daddy. Nobody says that any more.'

'What's a good expression?'

'Well . . . he resonates me.'

'Good Lord!'

'Please just set that stuff down, Daddy. I want to finish this one place first.'

He went over and put the sandwich and thermos on the sawhorse. As he was unbuttoning his shirt, he had his back to Nancy. He stopped, motionless, his finger tips touching the third button. Max Cady sat on a low pile of timbers twenty feet away. He had a can of beer and a cigar. He wore a yellow knit sports shirt and a pair of sharply creased slacks in a shade of cheap electric blue. He was smiling at Sam.

Sam walked over to him. It seemed to take a long time to walk twenty feet. Cady's smile didn't change.

'What are you doing here?' Sam kept his voice low.

'Well, I'm having a beer, Lieutenant, and I'm smoking this here cigar.'

'I don't want you hanging around here.'

Cady looked quietly amused. 'So the man sells me a beer and I'm thinking about maybe renting a boat. I haven't fished since I was a kid. Fishing any good in the lake?'

'What do you want?'

'That's your boat, hey?' He gestured with the cigar, winked with obscene significance and said, 'Nice lines, Lieutenant.'

Sam looked back and saw Nancy sitting on her heels, the short red shorts pulled to strained tightness around the young hips.

'God damn it, Cady, I—'

'A man has a nice family and a boat like that and a job where he can take off when he feels like it, it must be nice. Go out into the lake and mess around. When you're locked up you think of things like that. You know. Like dreaming.'

'What are you after? What do you want?'

The small deep-set brown eyes changed, but the smile still exposed the cheap white teeth. 'We started pretty near even back there in forty-three, Lieutenant. You had a fancy education and a commission and little gold bars, but we both had a wife and a kid. Did you know that?'

'I remember hearing you were married.'

'I got married when I was twenty. The boy was four when you got me sent up. I saw him when he was a couple weeks old. Mary dumped me after I got life. She never even visited. They make it easy to do when you're in for life. I signed the law papers. And I never got another letter. But my brother wrote me how she got married again. Married a plumber there in Charleston, West Virginia. Had a whole litter of kids. My brother sent me clippings when the kid got killed. My kid. That was in fifty-one. He was twelve, and he fell off his motor scooter under a delivery truck.'

'I'm sorry about that.'

'Are you, Lieutenant? You must be a nice guy. You must

be a real nice guy. I looked Mary up when I got back to Charleston. She damn near dropped dead when she recognized me. The kids were in school and the plumber was out plumbing. That was last September. You know, she'd got fat, but she's still a pretty woman. All the Pratt women are pretty. Hill people, from around Eskdale. I had to bust open the screen door to get to talk to her. Then she ran and got one of those fireplace things and tried to hit me over the head with it. I took it away from her and bent it double and threw it in the fireplace. Then she came out quiet and got in the car. She always had a mean temper.'

'Why are you telling me this?'

'I want you to get the picture, like I told you last week. I drove her over to Huntington—that's only about fifty miles—and that night I got in a booth with her while she called up the plumber. By then she was doing just what I told her, and I had her say she was taking a little vacation from him and the kids. I hung up while he was still yelling. I made her write me a love note and date it, asking me to take her away for a while. I made her write it full of dirty words. I stayed with her about three days in a hotel in Huntington. By then I got tired of her sniveling all the time and blubbering about her kids and her plumber. All the fight was gone, but she was marked up from that first day when she was still trying to get away. Are you getting the picture, Lieutenant?'

'I think so.'

'When I had enough of her, I told her that if she ever tried to yell cop, I'd mail a photostat of the note to the plumber. And I'd come around and see if I could throw a couple of the plumber's kids under some delivery trucks. She was impressed. I had to put damn near a whole fifth of liquor into her before she passed out. Then I drove her over the Big Sandy into Kentucky, and when I found one of those rough little roadhouses near Grayson, I lifted her out and put her in an old heap parked there. About a mile back up the road I threw her shoes and her dress in a field. I give her a good chance to work her way home.'

'This is supposed to scare me.'

'No, Lieutenant. This is just part of the picture. I had a lot of time to think. You know. I'd remember how it was when we got married. I'd gone back to Charleston on leave. I was twenty and it was 1939 and I had two years in. I wasn't fixing to get married, but she'd come into town with her folks on Saturday night. She was just turned seventeen and I could tell looking at them they were hill folk. My people came from around Brounland before they moved down into Charleston. I followed them around town, never taking my eyes off Betty. After lockup at night I'd remember how it was on that Saturday night, and how the wedding was, and how she came down to Louisiana when we had the maneuvers before I got shipped. She wanted to be near me. She was religious. Came from a big clan of Bible shouters. But it didn't stop her taking a big interest in climbing into the hay.'

'I don't want to listen to all this.'

'But you'll listen, Lieutenant. You want the word. I got this word for you. After I found out from my brother about her marrying again, I planned the whole thing, just exactly the way I did it. I changed it just a little. I was going to keep her a week instead of only three days, but she lost her fight too fast.'

'So?'

'You're supposed to be a big smart lawyer, Lieutenant.

I thought about her and naturally I thought about you.'

'And you made plans for me?'

'Now you're getting warm. But I couldn't make plans for you because I didn't know how you were set. I wasn't even sure I could locate you. I hoped to hell you hadn't been killed or died of sickness.'

'Are you threatening me?'

'I'm not threatening you, Lieutenant. Like I said, we started pretty near even. Now you're a wife and three kids ahead of me.'

'And you want us to be even again.'

'I didn't say that.'

They stared at each other, and Cady was still smiling. He looked entirely at ease. Sam Bowden could find no way to control the situation. 'Did you poison our dog?' he demanded, and immediately regretted asking the question.

'Dog?' Cady's eyes went round with mock surprise. 'Poison your dog? Why, Lieutenant? You slander me.'

'Oh, come off it!'

'Come off what? No, I wouldn't poison your dog any more than you'd put a plainclothes cop on my tail. You wouldn't do a thing like that.'

'You did it, you filthy bastard!'

'I've got to be careful. I can't take any punches at you, Lieutenant. I'd get sent up for assault. Want a cigar? They're good ones.'

Sam turned helplessly away. Nancy had stopped working. She was standing looking intently toward them, her eyes narrowed, and she was biting her underlip.

'There's a real stacked kid, Lieutenant. Almost as juicy as your wife.'

Sam turned back blindly and swung. Cady dropped

his beer can and caught the punch deftly in the palm of his right hand.

'You get one sucker punch in a lifetime, Lieutenant. You've had yours.'

'Get out of here!'

Cady had stood up. He put the cigar in the corner of his mouth and spoke around it. 'Sure. Maybe after a while you'll get the whole picture, Lieutenant.' He walked toward the shed, moving lightly and easily. He grinned back at Sam, then waved his cigar at Nancy and said, 'See you around, beautiful.'

Nancy came over to Sam. 'Is that him? Is it? Daddy! You're shaking!'

Sam, ignoring her, followed Cady around the shed. Cady got behind the wheel of an old gray Chevy. He beamed at Sam and Nancy and drove out.

'He *is* the one, isn't he? He's horrible! The way he looked at me made me feel all crawly, like worms do.'

'That's Cady,' he said. His voice was unexpectedly husky.

'Why did he come *here*?'

'To put a little more pressure on. God knows how he found out we'd be here. I'm glad your mother and the boys weren't here.'

They walked back to the boat. He glanced down at her as she walked beside him. Her face was solemn, thoughtful. This was not a problem that would affect only him and Carol. The children were within the orbit.

Nancy looked up at him. 'What are you going to do about it?'

'I don't know.'

'What is he going to do?'

'I don't know that either.'

'Daddy, do you remember a long time ago when I was little and the nightmares I had after we went to the circus?'

'I remember. What was the name of that ape? Gargantua.'

'That's right. The place where they had him had glass walls and you held me by the hand and he turned and he looked right at me. Not at any of the other people. Right at me. And I felt like something inside me curled up and died. It was something savage that didn't have any right to be in the same world I was in. Do you know what I mean?'

'Of course.'

'That man is a little bit like that. I mean I got a little bit of the same impression. Miss Boyce would say I was being unrealistic.'

'And who is Miss Boyce? I've heard that name.'

'Oh, she's our English teacher. She's been telling us that good fiction is good because it has character development in it that shows that nobody is completely good and nobody is completely evil. And in bad fiction the heroes are a hundred per cent heroic and the villains are a hundred per cent bad. But I think that man is all bad.'

Never before, he thought, have we been able to talk on an equivalent, adult level without a mutual shyness. 'I suppose I could understand him, if I wanted to. He was in a dirty, brutal business, and he was a combat-fatigue case, and he went right from that into life imprisonment at hard labor. And that is a brutalizing environment. I suppose he couldn't think of it as a reward for services rendered. So there had to be somebody to blame. And he couldn't blame himself. I became the symbol. He doesn't see me. He doesn't see Sam Bowden, lawyer, home owner, family type. He sees the lieutenant, the young J.A.G. full of puritanical righteousness who ruined his life. And I wish I could be one of your hundred per cent heroes about it. I wish I didn't have a mind full of reservations and rationalizations.'

'In our psychology class Mr. Proctor told us that all mental illness is a condition where the individual can't make a rational interpretation of reality. I had to memorize that. So if Mr. Cady can't be rational . . .'

'I believe he's mentally sick.'

'Then shouldn't he be treated?'

'The law in this state is designed to protect people from being wrongly committed. A close relative can sign commitment papers which will put a person away for a period of observation, usually sixty days. Or, if a person commits an act of violence or, in public, acts in an irrational manner, he can be committed on the basis of the testimony of the law officers who witness the violence or irrationality. There's no other way.'

She turned and ran her fingers along the sanded side of the hull. 'So there isn't much to do.'

'I would appreciate it if you'd break your date tonight. I'm not ordering you to. You would probably be safe, but we wouldn't know if you were safe.'

She thought it over, frowning. 'I'll stay home.'

'I guess we can break out the paint.'

'All right. Are you going to tell Mother about this?'

'Yes. She has the right to know everything that happens.'

Tommy Kent appeared a few minutes before Carol and the boys came back. He was a rangy, good-looking boy, polite, amusing and just deferential enough. He was given a brush. He and Nancy painted in the same area of the hull, each objecting to the other's sloppy work. Sam was glad to see how she handled him. No melting looks. No tinges of adoration. She was brusque with him, fencing with him with pert confidence and the sure-footedness of self-respect, quietly aware of her own attractiveness. Sam was surprised that her young weapons were so professionally edged and were wielded with such an air of long practice. She treated him like a slightly incompetent elder brother, which was, of course, precisely the correct tactics with a school wheel like Tommy Kent. Sam, giving them sidelong glances from his painting position near the bow, could detect only one flaw in her utter naturalness. She took no pose or attitude that was in any way ungainly or awkward. She was as careful as if she were dancing. He heard her break the date. She was just sufficiently apologetic to avoid being rude. And just vague enough to awaken suspicion and jealousy. Sam saw the black scowl on Tommy's face when Nancy turned away from him, and thought, Young man, she just sank the hook. She's keeping the rod tip up, and she's got the drag set perfectly. And when the time comes, she's going to be just as expert with the net, and you will flap in the bottom of the boat, eyes rolling and gill covers trembling. Pike Foster never had a chance, and now she's ready for bigger game.

After Carol arrived and made Nancy take time off for her sandwich and tea, and the four young ones were busily painting, Sam bought two beers and took Carol down to one of Jake's sagging docks and sat beside her, feet dangling just above the water. There he told her about Max Cady.

'Here!' she said, her eyes wide and round. 'Right here?'

'Right here, watching Nancy, when I got back. And when I looked at Nancy I seemed to see her the way he was seeing her and she'd never looked more undressed, even in that bikini thing you let her wear only when we're on the island without guests.'

She closed her fingers on his wrist with hysterical strength and shut her eyes tightly and said, 'It makes me feel ill. Oh, God, Sam! What are we going to do about it? Did you talk to him? Did you find out about Marilyn?'

'I talked to him. Right at the end I lost my temper. I tried to hit him. I was tremendously effectual. I tried to hit him while he was sitting down. I could have tossed a tennis ball at him. Underhand. His damn forearms are as big as my thighs, and he's as quick as a weasel.'

'How about Marilyn?'

'He denied it. But he denied it in a way that was the same as telling me he did it.'

'What else did he say? Did he make threats?'

For a moment Sam was tempted to keep the story of Cady's wife to himself. But he plodded through it, trying to do an unemotional job of straight reporting, looking down at the green bay water. Carol did not interrupt. When he looked at her it was as though she had suddenly, tragically become an older woman. At thirty-seven he had taken great pride in her agelessness, at the way she could look a consistent thirty and, at special times, a gay and miraculous twenty-five. Now, with shoulders slumped, and face all bones and gauntness, he saw for the first time how she would look when she became very old.

'It's hideous!' she said.

'I know.'

'That poor woman. And what a slimy way to threaten us. By indirection. Did Nancy find out who he was?'

'She didn't notice him until toward the end. When she saw us talking, she guessed. When I threw my ridiculous punch, she knew. After he drove away we talked. She made good sense. I think I'm very proud of her. She willingly broke tonight's date.'

'I'm glad. Isn't Tommy nice?'

'Quite nice, but don't start talking as if she's eighteen. He's better material than Pike. And she seems to be able to handle him well. I don't know where she learned.'

'It isn't something you learn.'

'I guess she inherited it from you, honey. There I was, minding my own business, looking around for a place to sit in that cafeteria and …' He was trying to be light, but he knew it was falling flat. Her head was bent and he saw the tears clinging to her black lashes. He put his hand on her arm.

'It will be all right,' he said. She shook her head violently. 'Drink your beer, baby. Look. It's Saturday. The sun is shining. There's the whole brood. We'll make out. They can't lick the Bowdens.'

Her voice was muffled. 'You go back and help. I'll stay here a little while.'

After he picked up his brush he looked back. She looked small out on the dock. Small, humbled and dreadfully afraid.

CHAPTER FIVE

He had met Carol on a Friday noon in late April of 1942 at the Horn and Hardart Cafeteria near the campus of the University of Pennsylvania. He was in his final year of law school. She was in her senior year in the undergraduate school.

Seeing no seats on the ground floor, he had carried his tray up the stairs. It was almost as crowded upstairs. He looked across the room and saw an exceptionally pretty girl alone at a wall table for two. She seemed to be reading a textbook. Had it happened a year earlier he would never have gone over and balanced the tray on the corner of the table and said, 'Do you mind?' He was not particularly shy, but at the same time he had always been awkward about approaching a girl he did not know. But it was 1942 and there was a new and reckless flavor in the world. Standards were changing quickly. He had been hitting the books hard, and it was April and there was the smell of spring, and this was a very pretty girl indeed.

'Do you mind?'

She gave him a quick, cool glance and looked back down at her book. 'Go ahead.'

He unloaded his tray and sat and began to eat. She had finished her lunch and was eating cheesecake, taking very small morsels onto her fork, making it last. As she showed no intention of looking up, he felt perfectly safe in staring at her. She was good to stare at. Long black lashes and good brow and high cheekbones. Curiously harsh black hair. She wore a green nubby suit and a yellow blouse with meager ruffles at the throat. He thought forlornly of some of his more extroverted friends, and how blandly and confidently they could open a conversation. Soon she would finish her cheesecake and coffee and be gone, perhaps with another cold little glance. And he could sit alone and think of what he should have said.

Suddenly he recognized the text she was reading. He had used it when he was an undergraduate. Durfey's *Abnormal Psychology*. After several mute rehearsals, he said with the greatest possible casualness, 'That course gave me a bad time.'

She glanced over at him, as though surprised to find someone at the table. 'Did it.' She looked back at her book. It was not a question. It was an end to all conversation.

He floundered on, saying, 'I ... I objected to the vagueness of the field. They use labels, but they don't seem to be able to measure ... things.'

She closed the book slowly, keeping her finger in it at her place. She stared at him and at his plate. He wished he had ordered something with more dignity than franks and beans.

'Don't you know the rules?' she asked frigidly.

'What rules?'

'The unwritten rules. You are not supposed to try to strike up a conversation with the coeds at this great university. We are drab, shabby, myopic little things you men students call bookbags. We're all beneath your lordly notice. If a dear fraternity brother makes the social error of bringing a bookbag to a fraternity function, he is looked on with loathing. So suppose you whiz on out to Bryn Mawr and try your luck out there.'

He felt his face turn sweaty red. She had opened her text again. His awkwardness turned slowly to anger. 'All right. So I spoke to you. If you don't want to talk, say so. But being pretty doesn't give you any special right to be rude. I didn't establish the unwritten rules. I don't date the coeds here because it so happens that I'm engaged to a girl in New York.'

There was no sign she had heard him. He stabbed at a frank and it jumped off the plate into his lap. As he replaced it she said, without looking up, 'Then why try to pick me up?'

'That's pretty damn arrogant, isn't it?'

She stared at him and pursed her lips. He saw that her eyes were so dark a brown they were nearly black. 'Is it?'

'Arrogant and also self-conscious. I have no intention of picking you up. And if I did have, brother, I'm cured.'

And she grinned at him, a wide gamin grin that mocked him. 'See? You admit you had the idea.'

'I did not!'

'It's almost impossible for most people in this world to be the least bit honest and candid. You certainly don't look the type.'

'I'm completely honest with myself.'

'I doubt it. Let's see if you can be. Imagine that when you came out with your forlorn little gambit, I'd risen like a hungry bass. And we have a real earnest talk about the course. Then you see I'm sort of toying with this cheesecake and then you go and get me some more coffee and I react as though you'd cut your way through a wall of human flesh to bring me emeralds. And then we leave together, and let's say you have a two-o'clock class and we've dawdled around so long you only have five minutes to get there. Now be honest. We stand out in front. And I say, with a suggestion of a simper, it's been so terribly interesting. This is your chance to be honest. Would you cut your two-o'clock just to walk me back to my sordid little dormitory?'

'Certainly not.' She looked at him with that infuriating smile. He searched his own mind. He sighed.

'Okay. Yes, I would. But there's something inaccurate and unfair about this.'

She put her hand out. 'Congratulations. You are quasi-honest. I'm Carol Whitney.' Her handshake was firm and she withdrew her hand quickly. 'And, for your additional information, I am engaged to a very wonderful guy who, at the moment, is down in Pensacola learning to fly. So there will be no simpers and no fluttering lashes.'

'Sam Bowden,' he said, smiling at her. He nodded at her book. 'That course gave me a rough time.'

'Nice recovery. I think I like you, Sam Bowden. I happen to be doing very well in it. How long ago was this rough time?'

'Couple of years ago. I'm in the law school now. Last year of it.'

'Then what?'

'Something to do with the war, I suppose. Claire insisted I finish out and get the degree, instead of doing what she called something foolish. Her father has a factory in Jersey and he's loaded with war contracts. Claire has been campaigning to have me go in with him. He's willing, and he guarantees a deferment. I haven't decided. We're going to be married as soon as I get the degree. Does everybody tell you a personal history?'

'I'm a sympathetic type. Bill and I are going to be married as soon as they pin the Navy wings on him. I'm no heiress to a defense plant in Jersey, but even if I was I couldn't keep him out of this thing. He's all hopped up. I guess I wouldn't try.'

He did get her more coffee and they did leave together and he said, 'I'll walk you to the sordid dormitory.'

'No flashy convertible?'

'Nope. I'm one of the laboring classes.' He fell in slow step with her. 'The first two years were gravy. Then my father died. With summer jobs and part-time jobs I've managed to hold on. I quit working for this last three months because I've got enough to finish out if I'm careful, and I want to put all the time I can into the books. It makes a funny situation when patriotism has to conflict with the dollar.'

'How do you mean?'

'My brother and I have to help support my mother. Her income isn't enough. He's got a wife but no kids. Mother lives with them in Pasadena. And George is about to get drafted. That's a good reason I couldn't trot off and sign up. The allotments from two G.I.s would be pretty slim.'

'So the Jersey plant looks good.'

'Or at least a commission if I could work it.'

'I haven't got a sou. I'm an only child. Mother died ten years ago. Dad is able to send enough to keep me going. He's worked in the oil fields all his life. Whenever he's been able to scrape enough together, he goes into a wildcat operation, and the holes are always dry, but he never gives up.'

When they reached her dormitory he asked the crucial question. She hesitated and then said, 'Yes, I'll be eating there tomorrow at the same time.'

By the end of a week they were spending every free moment together. They talked of everything under the sun. They told each other it was a perfectly platonic relationship. They told each other often of their love and loyalty for Bill and Claire. And they said Bill and Claire could not possibly object to an honest friendship between a man and a woman. Though he stole time from his books, his mind was quicker and fresher than it had ever been, and he could work with so much efficiency that he knew he was doing well. They had no money. But it was spring in Philadelphia and they walked endless miles and sat in parks and talked and talked and talked. Just an honest friendship. It was not significant that when he saw her walking toward him, his breath would catch in his throat.

He wrote and phoned Claire dutifully. She wrote to Bill and read him Bill's letters, and when she skipped over personal passages he was filled with a dark fury. He said Bill seemed like a nice guy. He was convinced Bill was a braggart, a mental lightweight, an incurable and perennial juvenile. As revenge he read Claire's perfumed letters to Carol. And was embarrassed at how superficial Claire sounded.

It came to the inevitable turning point in a small city park at midnight on a gentle, starry night in late May. They had talked about the war and about childhood and music and pine trees and the best breed of dog. Then she said she had an eight-o'clock and they stood up, facing each other, and her face was faintly illumined by a distant street lamp. There was a most curious silence and he put his hands on her shoulders. She moved vividly and completely into his arms and the long hungry kiss stirred them so they swayed and lost balance. They sat on the bench and he held her hand during a long and wonderful silence, while she tilted her head far back and looked directly overhead at the stars. They kissed again and their need and urgency increased until she pushed him gently away.

'It's going to be pure horror telling Bill,' she said.

'And Claire.'

'Pooh to Claire.'

'And to Bill. It's an easy math problem. We make two happy and two unhappy instead of four unhappy.'

'The world's oldest rationalization, darling.'

'Please say that again.'

'The world's old—'

'Just that last word.'

'Darling? Gosh, I've been calling you that for weeks, but not out loud. And there are lots of other words. Let's cover the whole list. You first.'

They stayed up all that night. They got their degrees. The rings were mailed back. They were married. They were utterly and sublimely convinced that no two people in the history of mankind had ever been more in love or more perfectly suited to each other in every way. It was a quiet civil wedding. An unexpected check from her father financed them while he sought and obtained a commission and reported to Washington for duty. The rented room in the brick house in Arlington was a special and personal heaven.

She went to the West Coast with him and they shared the three weeks he waited there at Camp Anza for shipment. George had been in the Army six months by then. Carol charmed Sam's mother and sister-in-law, and it was agreed she should move in with them rather than go to Texas to be with her father. She was seven months' pregnant when he left, and he was very glad she was with his mother and Beth.

He was shipped out in early May of 1943, and came

back to the States in September of 1945, Captain Bowden, deep brown from forty days on the blue canvas hatch cover of an A.P. – came back to a world much changed. George had been slain in Italy in 1944. And his mother had died two months later. Carol's father had died in an oil-field accident in Texas, and after burial expenses and sale of his possessions, there had been fifteen hundred dollars left. Sam requested and received his separation in California. He moved into the small rented house in Pasadena and became acquainted with his wife and the daughter he had never seen. Two weeks after he arrived they attended Beth's wedding. She married an older man, a widower who had been kind to the women living alone.

And two weeks later, after long phone conversations with Bill Stetch, they were in New Essex, in a rented house, and Sam was boning up for his bar examinations. And on Christmas Eve Carol announced, with mock outrage and pointed comments aimed at all military people in general and one Captain Bowden in particular, that she found herself a tiny bit pregnant.

Sam painted the hull of the boat in long strokes, half hearing the chatter of the children. Good years. The best of years. Much love, and a success that was gratifyingly steady though not in any special sense spectacular.

He was glad when Carol left the dock and began to work. Bucky, without anyone noticing, had decided to paint the underside of the hull. He had a big brush and he liked to get it full of paint. He had been painting directly over his head. Carol yelped when she saw him. Bucky was a uniform ghastly white, a clown in total makeup. They all stopped painting and got rags and turpentine and worked on Bucky. He was full of shrill resentment and wiggled incessantly. When he was reasonably clean, all the kids went over to change at the Boat Club and swim off the dock there. Carol and Sam finished the painting job.

On Monday morning, after he had finished his mail and switched some of his appointments around, Sam made an eleven-o'clock appointment with Captain Mark Dutton at New Essex Police Headquarters. Police Headquarters adjoined City Hall, and Dutton's office was in the new wing. He was Captain of Detectives, an ordinary-looking man in an ordinary gray suit. Sam had seen him two or three times before at civic functions. Dutton had gray hair and a quiet manner. He could have been a broker, insurance agent, advertising man – until he looked directly at you. Then you saw the cop eyes and the cop look – direct, skeptical and full of a hard and weary wisdom. The small office was neat. A glass wall looked out over a bull pen where more than half the desks were empty, and the walls were lined with tall gray files.

After they shook hands and Sam was seated, Dutton said, 'This is the same thing Charlie Hopper saw me about?'

'Yes. About Max Cady. Charlie seemed to think that you people would be able to ... badger him. I don't want to ask special favors, you understand. But I think he's dangerous. I know he's dangerous.'

'Charlie is a politician. The first aim is to make people happy. The second aim is to make people think they're happy.'

'You didn't promise him anything?'

'We pulled Cady in and held him while we checked.'

'Charlie told me. He isn't wanted anywhere.'

'No. Like they say, he's paid his debt to society. He can account for the car and the money. He's not indigent. Because of the nature of the only conviction on his record, we set up a card for him in the known-deviate file.'

'Captain, it's possible that he could be wanted somewhere. I mean if you could take some further action.'

'What do you mean?'

Sam recounted Cady's story of the abduction and rape of his ex-wife. With the precision of a trained legal mind he was able to recall and include all pertinent facts. Dutton pulled a scratch pad closer and made notes as Sam talked.

'No last name?' Dutton asked.

'No, but it shouldn't be difficult to find her.'

Dutton looked at his notes. 'She can be found. Let me ask you this. Do you think Cady was making this story up – to give you the shakes?'

'In my profession, Captain, I've listened to a lot of lies. I'd say he was telling the truth.'

Dutton frowned and tugged at his ear lobe. 'This is a shrewd animal you're dealing with. If it's the truth, he knows he gave you enough facts so she can be found. So he must be very damn well sure that she's too cowed to sign a complaint. Also, I've run into some of those hill people. They aren't inclined to go to the law for help even when they aren't cowed.'

'But you'll try it?'

'I'll put it up to the people in Charleston and ask them to see what they can do. There's a chance she never did go back home, you know. But she probably did. There's the kids. I wouldn't be too hopeful about this, Mr. Bowden.'

‘If it doesn’t work out, Captain, couldn’t you still force someone to leave town?’

Dutton nodded. ‘We’ve done it, not frequently. The last time was three years ago. This is a fairly clean town. Cleanest of its size in the state. That doesn’t mean spotlessly clean, Mr. Bowden. But it means that we’ve kept the syndicate type of operation out. We let a few small-time operators stay in business, because there’s always a certain level of demand. When they try to get too big, or when they try to move in on legitimate enterprise or rough up the taxpayers, we crack down quick and hard. When a syndicate operation tries to move in, we give our small-time operators protection. In return they contribute to both political parties and to the Police Benevolent Fund, and they keep us advised on any floaters who come to town and start looking around for a score. I’m speaking frankly and off the record. The proof can be found in the F.B.I. statistics. We have a low index in nearly every classification of crime. Twenty years ago we had one of the highest in the state. The Christer set continually tries to nail us for playing footsie with our tame rascals. We keep the little devil we know in business and keep out the big devil we don’t. But you can’t make them see that. It’s safe to walk the streets at night in New Essex. That’s enough for me. I know we’re doing a job. Three years ago two of the big Chicago-Miami-Las Vegas types rolled into town with their sunglasses, their pigskin luggage, their lavender Cadillac and a pair of the kind of blonde secretaries who can’t quite type. They took suites at the New Essex House and started to circulate. They wanted to sell syndication to our tame operators. Chief Turner and Mayor Haskill and Commissioner Goldman and I had ourselves a conference. We put ten of our best men on that quarter.

We interpreted the law our own way. Leave them alone and we'd have trouble. Big bad trouble.

'So we gave them trouble first. They couldn't turn around without breaking some ordinance they'd never heard of. We bugged both suites and that gave us some more leads. Both times the blondes left the hotel they were picked up and brought in and fined heavily for soliciting, and given the usual blood tests and physicals. You never saw two madder ex-showgirls. It took four days and fifty-six hundred dollars in fines before they gave up. We checked the route they took out of town and alerted the county boys and the state boys. They were grabbed four times for speeding before they hit the state line. Speeding and drunken driving. They all had licenses, and we lifted all but one so there'd be one driver left, one of the girls to get them over the state line. They haven't been back. But sooner or later somebody will try again. There's money here. And where there's money you can sell organized vice.'

'You couldn't do that to Cady?'

'It could be done. It would take a bunch of men and a lot of time. I checked him over myself while he was in the shop. He won't scare and you can't hurt his dignity because he hasn't got any.'

'Will you do it?'

Dutton balanced a yellow pencil on a thick index finger, looked sharply at Sam and said, 'No.'

'Can you give me a reason, Captain?'

'I can give you a lot of reasons. One: We're up to a hundred and thirty thousand population. We have the same size police force, in man power but not in equipment, that we had when there were eighty thousand. We're undermanned, underequipped, underpaid and overworked.

When something pops I have to call men back on duty and apologize to them because we can't pay all the overtime they have coming. The mothers keep marching on City Hall because we can't put more men at school crossings. Two: This is something that, as a lawyer, you can understand. It would set a curious precedent. We used extralegal methods and a lot of time and man power to avert a definite threat to the whole city, not to just one individual. Were we to do this, there would be questions asked. If he should employ the right shyster – forgive the term – it could get damn hot around here. The men I would assign would be very curious about this extra duty. Three: You are not a resident of this city. You work here, but your home is not here. You pay no city taxes. Your firm does, but this is not the business of your firm. As an individual, you pay no fractional part of my salary.'

Sam flushed and said, 'I didn't know it would sound—'

'Let me finish. Lastly, I got a look at the man. He looks clever. He doesn't seem to be in any murderous rage. I think he's just trying to pressure you a little. But I don't want you to go away from this office thinking you're getting no cooperation at all. If this Cady steps out of line anywhere inside my area of authority, I will see that the arresting officers and the judge are properly informed. And they will whack him with the stiffest deal the law allows.'

'Thank you very much, Captain. Have you got time to listen to what else he's done so far?'

'I'd be very interested.'

Sam told him about Sievers and about the dog.

Dutton leaned back and frowned and rubbed the eraser end of the yellow pencil against the side of his nose. 'If he made Sievers that fast and shook him that easy, then he's got a talent for the game. Do you have any proof about the dog?'

'No. But after talking to him, I'm certain.'

'That's outside our boundaries, of course.'

'I know that.'

Dutton thought a few more moments. 'I'm sorry, Mr. Bowden. I can't offer you any more than I've already told you I'd do. If you're genuinely alarmed about this, I suggest you pack your family off somewhere.'

'We've talked about that.'

'It might be a good idea. He'll get tired of his game and leave town after a while. Let me know any new developments.' He stood up and held his hand out. Sam thanked him and left.

At three in the afternoon, as he was passing Bill Stetch's office, he glanced in and saw that Bill was alone. On impulse he went in and told him the whole story. Bill was shocked and sympathetic and completely without any constructive suggestions. Sam had the curious feeling that Bill did not want to be pulled into the situation in any way. He had an air of holding himself apart.

'That poor, durn dog. There's some vicious people in the world, Sammy.'

'Cady is my special nomination.'

Bill leaned back, eyes thoughtful. He was a giant of a man, red face, pure white hair, blue eyes. His desk chair and his clothes were specially made. He had an air of bumbling joviality, but Sam had learned years ago, back in C.B.I. Headquarters, that Bill's manner concealed a mind that was intricate, devious and wonderfully shrewd.

'It puts you in a pretty uncomfortable position,' Bill said.

'And it's doing some funny things to me. I'll be damned if I could ever see myself going to the police and politely asking them to do something unlawful.'

Stetch chuckled. 'That old glamour girl holding those scales and taking a peek every little once in a while under her blindfold. And Samuel Bowden is her most avid worshiper. A lot of kids feel that way about it, but it's a damn rare man that can ... continue the infatuation.'

Sam felt that he was being patronized, and it annoyed him. 'What do you mean?'

'Don't get indignant, Sammy. Hell, when it was just Dorrity and Stetch, I knew we needed some noble motives around here, so we could retain our sanctimonious manner. After you worked with me in India I sensed you were our boy, and it couldn't have worked out better. Mike Dorrity and I are a pair of licensed pirates. We needed a balance wheel. One with starry eyes.'

'Now, dammit, Bill, I don't like—'

'Hold on. You're a partner. You do a hell of a fine job. You more than hold up your end. We're damn pleased we took you in. It was a smart move. But there's some parts of this business you can't handle, and we don't give you a chance to handle. Mike and I dirty our hands with that. It's the loophole division. We're well paid to find the loophole, regardless of the equities of the matter at hand.'

'Like that Morris option last year?'

'Just like that Morris option last year.'

'I thought that stank.'

'And it did, boy. That's why I took it away from you before you lost us a client. And handled it myself.'

'You make me feel like a damn neophyte.'

Bill shook his head. 'You're not. You're a smart attorney, Sammy. And you are a very rare article. You are a good man who believes in himself and what he is doing. Every law firm ought to have at least one in the shop. Too few do. So pay no attention to a cynical old bandit. We don't actually steal. Sometimes we show other people how they can steal, but it doesn't happen too often. Keep your regard for the lady with the scales. But don't get too appalled at yourself when you ask the police for an extralegal favor. Life is a continual process of compromise, Sammy. The idea is to come out the other end still clutching a few shreds of self-respect. End of lecture for today. I hope you solve your nasty little problem.'

When he was back in his own office, Sam sat behind his desk and thought of himself with contempt. The dreamer with the starry eyes. An amateur Abe Lincoln. Criminal lawyers made spirited defenses of known murderers. And were not thought unethical. So a man gave an option on land in good faith. Then he learns he can get more. So he comes in with his hat in his hand and says, 'Show me how this can be broken.' So you find a technicality and you break the option. He's a client. He pays for service.

But it was a contract made in good faith, and from the viewpoint of equity, the technicality is an absurdity.

Stop bleeding, Bowden. You're all grown up. Stop marching around waving all your little flags. Cady shoots your kids while you cry onto your diploma and look through all the dusty books for a way to slap his wrist legally.

He phoned Apex and left his number for Sievers.

At quarter to six as he was leaving, Sievers phoned and they made arrangements to meet in ten minutes at a bar three blocks from Sam's office. Sam phoned Carol and said he would be late. She said the children were all right, that Bucky had had another crying spell about Marilyn when he got home from school, but it didn't last long. All of them had gone to the creek with Jamie and Mike to find a stone. She had taken her big straw purse with her. They'd found a nice stone and had had a horrible time carrying it all the way back.

Sievers was standing at the bar when Sam walked in. He nodded and waited until Sam had a drink and then walked to a rear booth far from the jukebox and across from the men's room.

'I talked to Captain Dutton today. He won't do anything.'

'I don't see how he could. If you swung a hell of a lot more weight than you do, it might be managed. But he'd still be reluctant. By the way, he's top cop, that boy. Quiet and easy and hard as stones. Do you want to go ahead with what we talked about?'

'I . . . I think so.'

Sievers had a thin smile. 'No more talk about the legal way?'

'I've had enough of that kind of talk today to last me quite a while.'

'You're sharpening up.'

'Because of what has happened. Friday he drove out and poisoned my dog. The children's dog. There's no proof. Saturday he came to the boat yard, bold as brass.'

'He'll soften up.'

'Can you do what you said?'

'It can be done right for three hundred bucks, Bowden. I won't dig up the talent myself. I've got a friend. He's got the right contacts. He'll put three of them on him. I know the place, too. Out in back of 211 Jaekel Street. There's a shed and a fence near where he parks the car. They can wait in the angle of the shed and the fence.'

'What … will they do?'

'What the hell do you think? They'll beat hell out of him. With a couple of pieces of pipe and a bicycle chain, they'll do a professional job. A hospital job.' His eyes changed, became remote. 'I took a professional beating once. Oh, I was a hard boy. I believed that short of killing me they couldn't hurt me. I was going to bounce right back like Mike Hammer. But it doesn't work that way, Mr. Bowden. It marks you through and through. It's the pain, I guess. And the way they won't stop. The way you hear yourself begging and they still won't stop. The guts and the pride run right out of you. I wasn't worth a damn for two long years. I was perfectly healthy, but I had the jumps. I had them bad. I wasn't ready to have anybody start hurting me like that again. Then I started to come back. It happened eighteen years ago and even today I'm not sure I got all the way back to where I was. And I'm tougher than most. There isn't one man out of fifty – and understand, I've seen these figures work – who is ever worth a damn after a thorough professional beating. They have rabbit blood for the rest of their lives. You're doing the right thing.'

'There isn't any chance they might kill him by accident?'

'These are professionals, Bowden!'

'I know that. But it could happen.'

'Once in ten thousand times. Even so, we're clear. The orders go through too many channels. Even if anybody gave a damn, which they won't, it couldn't be tracked back to you.'

'Do I give you a check?'

'Good God, no! Cash. When can you put it up?'

'Tomorrow, as soon as the banks open.'

'Bring it here at the same time tomorrow. I'll begin to move on it tonight.'

'When do you think it will happen?'

'Tomorrow night or Wednesday night. No later.' He finished his drink, put his glass down and slid out of the booth.

Sam looked up at him and smiled crookedly and said, 'Does this sort of thing happen often? I'm pretty naïve, I guess.'

'It happens. People get too wise. They have to be straightened out, and sometimes this is the only way you can give them the word.'

'That's one of Cady's favorite expressions.'

'Then he'll be real pleased.'

'At what?'

'To get the word.'

He saved all three stories until both the boys were in bed and Nancy was in her room studying for her last exam of the year. Carol listened, her face quite still and remote. They sat side by side on the living-room couch. She sat with her legs folded under her, her round warm knee pressing against his thigh. She kept turning her silver bracelet around and around on her wrist.

'So you're going to pay three hundred dollars to have him beaten to within an inch of his life.'

'Yes. I am. But don't you see, it's the only—'

'Oh, darling, don't try to explain or apologize. I don't mean it that way. I'm gloating. I feel wonderful about it. I'd mow lawns and do other people's laundry to get that three hundred dollars.'

'I guess women are more primitive.'

'This one is. This one definitively is.'

He stood up restlessly. 'It's still a wrong thing to do. It's wrong that it should be possible to do a thing like this.'

'How?'

He shrugged. 'Suppose a disappointed client decided I needed similar treatment? If he had the right contacts, he could get the job done. It makes the world sound like a jungle. There's supposed to be law and order.'

She followed him and linked her arms around his waist and looked up at him. 'Poor Samuel! Darling, maybe it is a jungle. And we know there's an animal in the jungle.'

'I can't make myself clear. If this *is* the right way to handle it, then the foundations of my life are pretty creaky.'

She made a face. 'I'm creaky?'

'Only in places. I mean my professional life.'

'Can't you see, you great goose, that this isn't a logical situation? Logic leads you to a dead end. In a thing like this you proceed on instinct. And that's woman's best tool. And I know you did exactly the right thing. I would have done it. I wish I could have arranged it instead of you. You are a very good man, darling.'

'I am hearing that just a little bit too often.'

'You don't have to *growl* at me!'

'All right. I'm good man. I'm paying three hundred dollars to put another man in the hospital.'

'And you're still a good man. You suffer so much. Stop all the philosophical theories. Just help me rejoice because now I'm not afraid any more. And it is a very good thing not to be afraid. I'm a little bit afraid because it hasn't happened yet, but after it does, I am going to be the gayest wife in town. If that makes me a bloodthirsty witch, so be it.'

After Carol was asleep he got quietly out of bed and moved over to the chair by the bedroom window, pulled the blinds up with silent cautiousness, lighted a cigarette, and looked out toward the silvery road and the stone wall. The night was empty. His four incredibly precious hostages to fortune were in deep sleep. The earth turned and the stars were high. All this, he told himself, was reality. Night, earth, stars and the slumber of his family. And the other thing that had seemed so valuable was just a dusty and archaic code which enabled men to live closely together in reasonable peace and safety. In olden times the village elders punished those who broke the taboos. And all of the law was a vast, top-heavy superstucture built on the basic idea of the group enforcing the punishment of the nonconformist. It was a tribal rite, with white wigs, robes and oaths. It just did not happen to apply to his own situation. Yet two thousand years ago he could have sat in council with the elders and explained his peril and gained the support of the village, and the predator would be stoned to death. So this action was a supplement to the law. Thus it was right. Yet when he got back into bed, he still could not accept his rationalization.

CHAPTER SIX

Sievers made no report on Wednesday, and Sam could find nothing in the paper. On Thursday morning at nine-thirty he received a call from Dutton.

'This is Captain Dutton, Mr. Bowden. I got some news for you on your boy.'

'Yes?'

'We got him for disorderly conduct, disturbing the peace and resisting arrest. He got into a fight last night at about midnight in the yard in back of that rooming house on Jaekel Street. Three local punks jumped him. They marked him up pretty good before he got untracked. One got away and two are in the hospital. He threw one through the side of a shed and gave him a sprained back and multiple bruises. The other one's got a broken jaw, a broken wrist, concussion, and some ribs kicked loose. They laid his cheek open with a bike chain and thumped him around the eyes with a hunk of pipe.'

'Will he be put in jail?'

'Definitely, Mr. Bowden. He was dazed, I guess, and it was dark in the yard, and he swung on a patrolman when he came running across the yard and gave him a nose as flat as a sheet of paper. The second patrolman dropped him with a night stick and they took him in and got his face sewed and then brought him in and threw him in the tank. Judge Jamison has night court this week, and we'll see what we can give him tonight. He's yelling for a lawyer. Want the job?'

'No thanks.'

'Judge Jamison doesn't cooperate as much as some of the others, but I think he'll lay it on pretty good. Drop around tonight about eight-thirty and you can see how he makes out.'

'I'll be there. Captain, is it too early to ask you how they made out in Charleston?'

'No. It came out like I figured. The woman was contacted at her home by the Charleston police. She admitted she was married to Cady at one time, and claims she has not seen him since he was sentenced. She told them she didn't know he had been released. Too bad.'

'Thank you for trying.'

'Sorry more didn't come of it, Mr. Bowden.'

Sievers phoned at four and asked Sam to meet him in the same place. Sam arrived first. He took his drink back to the same booth and waited. When Sievers arrived he sat across from Sam and said, 'You should get a refund.'

'What happened?'

'They got careless. I sent word down the line that monkey was rugged. They gave him some love taps and when he didn't go down, they tried to love-tap him some more. And suddenly it was very much too late. And he purely scared the living hell out of those boys. The one that ran got hooked in the gut first. He can't breathe right yet, I hear. The word is going around. It's going to be hard to line up boys for a second shot at him. I hear that when one of them went through the shed wall it sounded like a bomb going off. I'm sorry it was handled so badly, Mr. Bowden.'

'But he will go to jail.'

'And he will be released.'

'Then what do I do?'

'I guess you pay for another treatment. You better set aside a thousand for this one. He isn't going to be caught napping a second time.'

By the time Sam got home Carol had most of the information from the evening paper, a single paragraph on a back page that gave the names of the two in the hospital and told of Cady's arrest.

'Are you going in?'

'I don't know.'

'Please go in and find out, darling.'

Night court was crowded. Sam sat in the back. There was a continual mumbling and shuffling of feet, a constant coming and going, so that he could not hear a word of what was going on. The ceiling was high, and naked bulbs made stark shadows. Judge Jamison was the most bored-looking human being Sam had ever seen. The benches were narrow and hard, and the room smelled of cigars, dust and disinfectant. When he saw a chance he moved up into the third row from the front railing. Cady's case came up at nine-fifteen. One of the city prosecutors, Cady, a young lawyer Sam had seen at bar-association meetings but whose name he couldn't recall, and two uniformed patrolmen lined up before the judge.

Sam, strain as he might, could catch only a word here and there. Cady's lawyer, in an earnest undertone, seemed to be stressing the fact that the attack had taken place on property where Cady rented his room. The patrolman with the bandaged nose testified in a blurred monotone. When the noise in the courtroom rose to too high a level the judge would rap indolently with his gavel.

The prosecutor and the defense lawyer talked animatedly, ignoring the judge for a time. Then they both nodded. The judge yawned, rapped the gavel again, and pronounced a sentence Sam could not hear. Cady walked over with his lawyer and paid money to a clerk behind a small desk. A bailiff started to lead him toward a side door, but Cady stopped and looked back, apparently searching the courtroom. Tape was a vivid diagonal white across his cheeks. His brows were swollen and bluish. Sam tried to shrink down on the bench, but Cady spotted him, raised one hand, smiled, and said quite audibly, 'Hiya, Lieutenant. How's it going?'

And he was led out. Sam spoke to three people before he could find out what had happened. Cady had pleaded guilty to striking the officer. The other two charges had been dismissed. He was sentenced to pay a hundred-dollar fine and spend thirty days in city jail.

He took the news back to Carol. They tried to believe it was good news, but it wasn't very comforting. Their smiles were stiff and faded easily. But, at the very least, it was thirty days of grace. Thirty days without fear. And thirty days of anticipation of the fear to come. As far as their morale was concerned, Cady could not have planned it better.

School had ended. The restrictions on the children were lifted. The golden summer had begun. Cady's thirty days began officially on the nineteenth of June. He would be released on Friday, the nineteenth of July.

They had planned that Nancy would go again to summer camp, and she had pleaded to be allowed to attend for six weeks this year instead of the usual month. It would be her fourth year at Minnatalla, and probably her last. The six weeks would begin on the first day of July.

Jamie would return for his second year to Gannatalla, the boys' camp that was three miles away and under the same management. The camps were on the shore of a small lake in the southern part of the state, a hundred and forty miles from Harper. Camp plans had been settled in family council back in April when the applications had to be in. After consideration of all factors, Nancy's request for six weeks had been granted. Then Jamie had objected strenuously to being limited to one month. It was pointed out to him that Nancy had been allowed to stay but one month when she was his age. He settled for a guarantee that when he was fourteen he would be allowed to register for six weeks. Bucky had been stolidly indignant about the whole thing. It meant nothing at all to him that he would start going in three years. Three years was half his entire age. It was an eternity. He was an unwilling victim of cruel and unnecessary discrimination. Everybody would be gone.

When he was at last resigned to a fate of staying home all summer he came up with a series of firm opinions about camps. They were crummy places. You had to sleep in the rain. The horses would kick you and the boats all leaked, and if you didn't wash six times a day, they beat you and beat you.

After the arrangements had all been made, Nancy had slowly begun to change her mind about it as summer approached. She was changing in body and emotions from child to woman. It was obvious from her attitude that she had begun to think of summer camps as kid stuff. A lot of the gang would be around Harper all summer. She named boys who were going to work on the new road job, a super-highway that was in the process of construction and would cross Route 18 three miles north of Harper. She thought maybe she could get a job in the village. But Sam and Carol thought it would be best for her to extend her childhood through one more summer of swimming, riding, handicraft, cookouts, hikes and singing around the bonfires.

Nancy was not sullen, and she was not a whiner. When it was made clear to her that she was going to go, she went into what Sam called her duchess condition. It was a majestic and patronizing aloofness, punctuated by telling sighs and barely audible sniffs. She was above all of them and, of course, would condescend to go along with their ideas, no matter how childish they were.

But at some point during the week after Cady was sentenced, there was a startling change of attitude. Nancy became vibrant about the plan, excited, going about with tiptoe pleasure. The change intrigued Sam and Carol.

One night Carol said to Sam, 'Mystery solved. I got her cornered today. She was packing her red dress, and with a furtive little manner about the whole operation. So I told her that would be a divine getup for scrabbling up the side of a mountain. So she told me firmly and haughtily that there are social evenings when the groups from both camps mingle. So I told her I was quite aware of that, and I was also aware that the top age for the young gentlemen from Gannatalla was fifteen, and thus the red dress would be like shooting a cricket with a deer rifle. Rather than be accused of lowering her sights, she confessed that Tommy Kent has a job as assistant director of athletics this year at Gannatalla.'

'Ho!'

'Yes, indeed. Ho! And the campers are closely supervised, and the female staff members of Minnatalla are not so closely supervised, and her Tommy will probably become very buddy with an elderly staff member of eighteen or so and break our chicken's heart.'

'It's a calculated risk. But I'm glad the duchess routine is over anyway. She'll be fifteen on the twentieth. What day does that come on?'

'A Saturday this year. We can drive down, bearing gifts.' She paused and gave him a stricken look. 'I didn't think before. That's the day after ...'

'I know.'

'What about them down there? Jamie and Nance. Will they be safe?'

'I suppose he could find out where they are. Almost any contemporary in the village would know where they go. I've thought about that. You know how it is down there. They travel in packs. Great yelping packs, full of muscular enthusiasm. I've planned to instruct the kids and have a talk with the management when we drive them down. But having Tommy there may simplify it. I can talk to him. I think I like that kid. There's a look of competence about him.'

'You'll have to hurry, then. They have a date tonight, and he leaves early in the morning. He has to get there early to help get the camp ready. They're going to the benefit barn dance at the firehouse. He's picking her up at eight.'

'I never knew this routine was going to start so soon.'

'We gals with Indian blood grow up early.'

That evening Nancy raced through her dinner and was ready by quarter to eight. Sam cornered her in the living room. 'Very rustic,' he said, approvingly.

'Do I look all right?'

'What are those things called?'

'These? Ranch jeans for girls. They're cut sort of like men's.'

'Sort of. But just to humor the idle curiosity of your senile male parent, just how do you get into them?'

'Oh, that's easy! See on the side of the legs here? Concealed zippers from your knee to your ankle.'

'Very effective with that shirt. It looks like a tablecloth from an Italian restaurant. Nance, honey, I assume you've told Tommy about our … problem.'

'Heck, yes!'

'When he arrives do you mind pretending you're not ready yet? So I can have a little chat with him?'

'The car will be loaded with kids, Daddy. What do you want to say to him? I mean I don't want you to sound—'

'I'll get him away from the others, honey, and I will not shame you.'

There was still some sun at eight o'clock when Tommy arrived, and the long summer dusk was beginning to gather in blue shadows under the trees. Sam came down from the porch and met Tommy when he was halfway across the yard from the driveway.

'Farmer Brown, I presume,' Sam said. Tommy wore bib overalls, a blue work shirt and a straw hat.

'Pretty corny outfit, isn't it, sir?'

'A proper uniform for the occasion. Nancy will be ready in a few minutes. I want to talk to you a minute, Tommy.'

He saw a fleeting look of apprehension and for a moment he knew exactly what Tommy was thinking. A sticky little scene coming up, with the papa saying how young his little girl was, and don't keep her out late and so on.

'Yes, sir?'

'Nancy says she's told you about a man who is giving us a bad time?'

'Yes, she told me. I can't remember his name. Brady?'

'Cady. Max Cady. In jail now. But he'll be released next month on the nineteenth. You're old enough so I can lay it on the line. I think the man is dangerous. I know he is. He wants to hurt me through my family. That's the way he could hurt me the worst. He may go down to camp. I want to give you an extra responsibility. I want to tuck Jamie under your wing. Make sure he isn't ever alone. Give the other people down there the word. I think you could achieve the best degree of alertness down there if you tell them there's been a kidnap threat. My wife and I talked this over, and we think he'll be safer there than here. Are you willing to do this?'

'Yes, sir. But what about Nancy?'

'You'll be three miles away from the other camp. I'm going to talk to them when we take the kids down. She's older than Jamie and less likely to forget to be cautious. But I think . . . she's a more logical target. I'm going to try to handle the problem here when Cady is released. If it is handled, I'll get word to you at once, Tommy.'

'I understand there aren't many men over at Minnatalla,' Tommy said dubiously.

'I know that. You will see Nancy off and on, I assume. Keep reminding her to stay with the pack. She's seen Cady. That's going to be a lot of help to her.' He gave Tommy a detailed description of the man and said, 'If a situation should come up, don't try to be impulsive and heroic. You're husky and you're an athlete, but you'd be no match for the man. He's got the size and speed and ruthlessness of a bear. And I don't think you could stop him with a pipe wrench.'

‘I understand.’

‘And understand this too. I’m not being dramatic.’

‘I know that, sir. I know about the dog. I never heard of anything like that before. I’ll make certain they’ll both be all right, Mr. Bowden. I won’t goof it.’

‘I know you won’t. Here comes the farmer’s lady.’

He watched them walk out to the parked car. There were long whistles as Nancy approached the car. After they left, waving and yelling, Sam went back to the porch.

When Carol came out, bringing him the unexpected bonus of a tall gin and tonic, he said, ‘I’m thinking about pendulums.’

She sat on the railing near him. ‘Lecture by Bowden.’

‘You can always tell, can’t you?’

‘Of course, darling. Your voice gets a little bit deeper and you articulate more carefully. Out with it.’

‘If I could rehearse this, it would be better. I suspect we’re near the end of the glamour days of juvenile delinquency. I think a very unusual crop of kids is coming along. Good kids, but strange. They’ve become bored with the dissipations of their elders and the animal philosophies of their contemporaries. They are tired of using the bogeyman of military service as a built-in excuse for riot and disorder. This is a very moral crop of kids. They are sophisticates, but they practice moderation by choice. They seem to have a sense of moral purpose and decent goals, which, God knows, are all right. But they appall me a little. They make me feel like a doddering degenerate. Tommy is a good kid. The pendulum is swinging back.’

She put her glass down carefully on the railing and clapped solemnly. ‘Hear, hear.’

‘Now stop listening to me and we will sit in this stagy dusk and listen to bugs.’

'To myriad insects, please.'

'You can tell temperature from crickets.'

'So you have told me a hundred times.'

'Another sign of senility. Banality and repetitiousness. And forgetfulness, because I never can remember the formula you use on a cricket.'

'Let's just say when the crickets sing outdoors, it's warm enough.'

'Fine.'

They sat in silence while night came. Jamie and some of his friends were playing in the barn. The shrilling of their voices merged with the insects' song. Sam tried to submerge himself completely in the subtle rhythms of the summer night, but he could not halt the ticking of the clock in the back of his mind. Each second brought them closer to the return of danger. And he knew that Carol too listened to that clock. It was, he thought, somewhat like the knowledge of a mortal illness. It made the immediate beauties more vivid, all pleasures sharper, while at the same time it stained beauty and pleasure with a distressing poignancy.

When the phone rang Carol went in and answered it and came back out and said, 'It's dispersal time. Go and break up the atomic set, darling.'

'Atomic?'

'Where have you been? They are constructing an atomic sports car.'

He broke up the group. Bicycle lights went up the road and plans for tomorrow were shouted back and forth. It was the wonderful world of all the summers of childhood. Television, after having been a source of worry for a time, was back under control. Summer was time to use the big muscles, time for running and yelping. Summer was the time when the big red dog should have been running with them, banging into tanned legs and knocking them down, undergoing a quavering ride in the atomic sports car, barking with frustration at being unable to join them in a tree, collapsing loose-jointed into her corner at night to enter a dream world that set her legs twitching while she ran with consummate valor after all the monsters she had terrified into flight.

They left early for camp on Monday, the first of July. Most parents would have taken the kids down on Sunday, and that had been the original plan, but after family debate, Sam had decided to take Monday off so that on Sunday they could picnic on the island. It had been a perfect day on the island. On the way home a stiff breeze had come up, and Bucky, accepting his Bonamine a little too late, had spent the last half hour of the trip home hanging over the rail, intensely indignant with his own stomach, aware of black betrayal.

In the early morning, excitement had closed Jamie's stomach into a knot. He could not eat. Lists were checked. Mike Turner came down the road to bid Jamie a forlorn farewell. The wagon was loaded, the house locked, and they took off. Bucky was infected by the excitement of the others, but on the way back home he would be sunk in sour gloom until, inevitably, he would fall asleep on the back seat.

They arrived at eleven, going to Minnatalla first despite Jamie's protestations so shrill and bitter that he had to be squashed firmly. The busy morning schedule was in frantic swing. Nancy's friends of other summers waved and called to her. After Sam and Jamie had off-loaded Nancy's gear into her cabin, he drove to the administration cottage and had a talk with the camp supervisor, a new man, younger than the man he had replaced. It was not a very satisfactory talk. The man's name was Teller. Sam soon recognized the type. Teller was very much like that sort of officious social worker who considers the rules and forms more important than the human beings he deals with. He was gently patronizing, and it was clear that he thought he was dealing with an over-protective parent.

'Nancy has a very good record here at Minnatalla, Mr. Bowden. We're delighted she's back with us, and I am certain she will have a happy and profitable summer.'

'I'm sure she will, Mr. Teller, but that isn't the point,' Sam said patiently. 'I'm concerned with her physical safety.'

'All our campers are carefully supervised, Mr. Bowden. They're busy every moment of the day. Lights-out is strictly enforced, and we have a very competent night watchman who makes a tour of the entire camp area four times a night. We permit all wearers of the Minnatalla merit button to go into Shadyside on Saturday afternoons. One of the staff supervises the junior campers, but the senior girls can—'

Sam interrupted, sensing how he must deal with Teller. 'She has been coming here for some time. This is her fourth year. I imagine that I am almost as familiar with all these details as you are. Nancy is not to go into Shadyside at any time.'

Teller looked pained. 'But surely that is unfair to the child, Mr. Bowden. When she sees others being given permission—'

'Nancy is perfectly willing to forgo those trips. She is . . . mature enough to recognize the fact she may be harmed.'

Teller flushed. 'I do not know how wise it is to frighten a child, Mr. Bowden.'

'I haven't made a special study of it myself. Are we in agreement? No trips to Shadyside for Nancy?'

'Yes, Mr. Bowden. I'm sure that if she has any errands, she can find someone who will be willing to make purchases for her.'

'I'm sure she can find a couple of dozen who will be willing. She's not an unpopular child.'

'I'm sure of that.'

The situation at Gannatalla was more reassuring. After Jamie was unloaded and fed into the schedule, Sam looked up Mr. Menard. He recognized Sam from the previous year. 'Hello, Mr. Bowden. Glad to have Jamie back.'

'I wanted to talk to you about—'

'A possible kidnaping deal? Tommy Kent gave me the word. I've advised everybody on the staff. I told them how to handle it. We won't treat Jamie differently than we treat anybody else. But, without being obvious about it, we're going to keep a special eye on him, and be on the lookout for anybody hanging around. We don't want you people worrying about him. There's no need to. And I'm going to talk to him about how he can cooperate.'

'I certainly appreciate this. Over there at the female department, Mr. Teller made me feel as if he thought I was making the whole thing up.'

'Bert is new and he's taking himself a little seriously right now. He was a playground supervisor. Actually, he's a lot better with kids than you'd expect. The kids will whip him into shape in a week, and as soon as I get a chance, I'll have a little talk with him.'

'I'll appreciate that very much. This sort of thing ... isn't very good for the nerves.'

'Anybody who goes after a man's kids hits him where he lives. God knows there's enough things to worry about that can happen to them accidentally. My pet nightmare is one of them drowning. I keep the staffers counting heads every minute of the swim periods.'

'Tommy Kent seems to be a good kid.'

'I'll let you know in a month. We get so many that start out just fine. Work like horses until the novelty wears off. Then they're more trouble than they're worth. If Kent can sustain it, he's a gem.' Menard winked at Sam. 'And do I detect more than a casual concern about the Bowden girl?'

'I think so.'

'Stay to lunch with us today?'

'Thanks, but we have to head back, Mr. Menard. We'll be back on the twentieth anyway, and probably on the thirteenth too.'

On the way home, after Bucky was asleep, Carol said, 'I know it has to happen, but I hate to cut the family down, really. It does make life a lot easier. But it makes it emptier too. I dread the time when they'll all be gone. I think about it during the day sometimes, and the house seems twice as empty.'

'You can delay that day, friend wife.'

'How?'

'With a little diligence and cooperation, I think I could fix it so that ... Hmmmm ... you're thirty-seven. Assume it would go away to school at eighteen. Nineteen plus thirty-seven. Yes, dear, you could be fifty-six before the house empties out completely. That is, provided we get to work on the project immediately.'

'Lascivious wretch! Beast!'

'Just finding out?'

She sat closer to him. A dozen miles went by. She said thoughtfully, 'We all get so playfully cynical about another b-a-b-y. Jokes about the diaper service and the PTA. You know, if this … this Cady thing wasn't happening to us, I'd like to have another.'

'Do you mean that?'

'I think so. Even with waddling around all stuck out in front and all the sterilizing and night feedings and later on watching it so it won't fall and all that. Yes, I think so. Because they're all so different. You think about what the next one would be like. Our three are – I don't know how to say it – they're all people.'

'I know what you mean.'

'And making people is a special thing. It's a special and a frightening responsibility.'

'You said Bucky was the last.'

'I know. And I said it for three years. And then I stopped saying it.'

'You're no bride, darling, even though you quite frequently manage to look like one.'

'The others were easy.'

'You didn't say so at the time.'

'Pooh! They were easy for us Indians.'

'Twenty minutes later you're back beading moccasins.'

'Nancy would be stricken with horror. And our friends would leer at each other and talk about carelessness.'

'But you still would go through with it?'

'Not now. Not while … we don't know.'

'We will know, I think. Before long.'

'And when this is over, we'll talk about it again, dear?'

'We'll talk about it again.'

'You should have something to say. It ties you down too. It changes your life.'

'When it comes to the point where I can't remember all their names, I'll bring you to a quivering halt.'

They were home by four. Bucky rose up in stuporous condition and drunk-walked to the house. The sky was dark and low and the clouds that hurried by seemed just above the tops of the elms. The wind was gusty and humid. It rattled the windows of the house. The house had a feeling of emptiness. When, at six, the heavy rains came, Sam backed the wagon out into the drive so the rain would wash the dust of the trip from it.

July had come too quickly. And nineteen days could not be made to last.

CHAPTER SEVEN

Sievers phoned Sam on Monday morning, July eighth, and came up to his office at ten-thirty.

'Something has come up,' he said. 'They haven't given me much notice, as usual. I'm being transferred. California. I head up one of the Apex agencies out there. It's a promotion.'

'Congratulations.'

'Thanks. It won't be possible for me to arrange the deal we were talking about. I mean, if you decided to go ahead with it.'

'I was going to. Can't you arrange it before you go?'

'Too far ahead. But I did a little fixing for you. Want to write this down? Joe Tanelli, 1821 Market. It's a candy-and cigar store, and a small-time horse room in the back. He'll expect you on Wednesday the seventeenth. Don't give him your name. Mention my name. He'll know the score. He'll want five hundred down. That's all right. Give it to him. And he'll want the other five after it's been taken care of. He'll round up better talent than last time.'

To Sam the situation was curiously unreal. He had not thought such a conversation possible in his office. And there was nothing particularly conspiratorial about Sievers' attitude. He could have been talking about the best place to buy fresh eggs.

'I appreciate this.'

Sievers took on the look of a man thinking back across the years. 'It used to be easier long ago, in other places. You take Chicago or Kansas City or Atlanta or Birmingham in thirty-three or thirty-four. The rates were cheap. Ten bucks for a broken leg. And a tops of two hundred if you wanted somebody killed and they weren't important. There's only a handful of killers for hire now in the whole country and they're on retainer for the syndicate. Even if you could contact them, the price would be up in the clouds. A hopped-up kid can be bought for less, but the job would be bungled. The pros do a clean job. Come in by plane with a good cover story. Two or three of them. Rent a legitimate car. Stay in a good hotel. Pick the time and the place and do it fast and clean and then get out. An amateur always gets caught and always sucks in the guy who hired him.'

Sam's polite laugh sounded forced and hollow. 'I haven't been thinking along those lines, Sievers.'

Sievers came back out of his memories and looked at Sam. 'I don't want to make you any more nervous than you are, Mr. Bowden, but I might as well tell you this. Just out of curiosity I had Apex in Wheeling run a check on him. When there's no specific client, it's done as a courtesy between branch offices. The Cadys are old stock. Hill people. There were four brothers, two older than Maxwell and one younger. Max Cady had no record prior to the Army sentence, but he wasn't any angel. None of the Cady boys were. Max got in the Army after he cut a man badly with a broken bottle. It was a fuss over a woman. The court gave him the choice of enlisting or going to prison, so he enlisted. The old man was in and out of prison his whole life. He was a moonshiner with a violent temper. He died of a stroke three years ago. He married the boys' mother when she was fifteen and he was nearly thirty. She's living with the youngest brother and she's been feebleminded her whole life. The oldest brother was shot to death eight years ago in a running gun battle with federal agents. The next oldest was killed in a prison riot in Georgia. He was serving a life sentence for felony murder. My pride was hurt when I did so bad tailing him. Now I don't feel so bad. He's one of the wild ones. They don't think the way people do. He was headed for jail whether he got caught on that rape charge or not. People like that have no comprehension of right and wrong. Their only thought is whether or not they'll be caught. Anything you can get away with is worth doing.'

'Isn't there a word for that?'

'Psychopathic personality. They make us learn the terms. But that's a classification where they put people they don't know what else to call. People they can't treat. People who don't respond to any appeal you can make to them. Except maybe the one we're trying to make.' He stood up. 'I've got a lot of stuff to clean up before I take off in the morning. Joe will fix it up for you.'

It was a long time after Sievers left before Sam could get his concentration back on his work. He respected Sievers for giving him all the unpalatable facts, but they served to make Cady even more ominous than he had been thus far. It was like when you were a child and a frightening shadow seemed to grow larger and blacker and more threatening as you watched it. He told himself Cady was human and vulnerable. He told himself it was shameful to be frightened of a man. And he decided there was no point at all in telling Carol what Sievers had learned. He would tell her of the new arrangement, but she needed no new reasons to be afraid of Cady.

On Friday, the twelfth of July, after the dinner dishes were done, Sam looked up from his book when he heard Carol make an odd sound. She was sitting on the couch, reading the paper. She lowered the paper and stared at him with an odd expression.

'What's the matter?'

'What was the name of the man you have to see next Wednesday night?'

'Tanelli. Joe Tanelli.'

'Come and look at this.'

He sat beside her and read the obituary of a Joseph Tanelli, age 56, address 118 Rose Street, who had died the previous night in Memorial Hospital of a heart attack. Mr. Tanelli had been a retail merchant in New Essex for the past eighteen years. There was a very long list of his survivors.

'It's probably not the same one, dear.'

'But what if it is?'

He spoke confidently. 'Even if it is, I can make a contact with somebody else at the address Sievers gave me.'

'Are you sure?'

'Practically positive.'

'I don't think you ought to wait until Wednesday, dear. I think you ought to go in tomorrow night.'

'Don't we have to go to the Kimballs' party?'

'I can go alone and you can meet me there.'

'I'll drive in tomorrow afternoon.'

'In the afternoon? It seems like something you ought to do at night, somehow.'

'I can find out what the score is in the afternoon at least. If it's the same man.'

But underneath his assurance he knew it was the same man. A malicious fate was dealing Cady every joker in the deck.

It was brutally hot on Market Street at four in the afternoon. Sam found a meter in the eighteen-hundred block and carefully locked the car. It was a neighborhood where you automatically locked the car. Number 1821 had no sign showing ownership or management. The door was two steps below sidewalk level. The small show window, almost opaque with dust, displayed a few weary soft-drink posters and cigar ads. In peeling gilt across the window was painted CIGARS MAGAZINES CANDY. That side of the street was in shade. A half dozen stone steps went up to the entrance of the neighboring building. A grossly fat woman with red hair sat on the top step. Her suety body bulged the soiled pink dress she wore. She took small sips from a can of beer.

He went down and tried the door, but it was locked.

'It's locked on account of Joe, honey,' a loud brassy voice informed him. He looked up into the round face of the fat woman. She was younger than he had guessed from his quick glance at her. 'That's right. Joe up and died. Somebody did him out of a dime and his heart give out on him from shock.' She giggled.

He went back up onto the sidewalk and looked at her. 'Have you any idea when they'll open up again?'

'Hell, they're open. It's just the front door locked sort of like a courtesy to Joe. You know. I don't know who's running it or who'll take over permanent, but they won't miss out on a day's action, especially a Saturday.'

He realized she was happily tight. 'How do I get in?'

'Now, if you want to get in, Doc, you go down there to the first alley and go back through the alley and take a left and count three doors and knock on the third one. But those horses will nibble you to death every time. Now just suppose you had twen'y bucks to kick away. It so happens there's a cute little blondie right in this building that's dying from being bored. You see, she's a singer with a band and the band folded and she's got to make a stake so she can get out to the Coast where she's got a tryout lined up. She's an honest-to-God college girl and—'

'No, thanks. Not today.'

She scowled at him. 'Horse players,' she said. 'Lousy horse players.'

He thanked her and followed her instructions. It was a door of heavy construction, with no window in it. It opened six inches and a round white face of uncooked dough with raisin eyes looked out at him and said, 'Yah?'

'I ... I want to talk to whoever is in charge.' He could hear a rumble of voices beyond the door.

'What about?'

'I ... Sievers sent me.'

'Hold on.' The door closed. A full minute passed. It opened again. 'Nobody ever heard of no Sievers.'

'Joe Tanelli knew him.'

'That's great.' The raisin eyes seemed to be looking through him and beyond him.

'Suppose ... I wanted to get a bet down.'

'Go to a track.'

'Wait a minute ...' But the door had closed firmly. He waited a few minutes and then knocked again.

'Now look, friend,' the white face said.

'Listen to me. Joe was going to do something for me.

Now he can't. But I still want it done and I still want to pay for it, and I want to know who to see.'

'Me. So what was it?'

'I can't stand here in the alley and tell you.'

'Look, Mack. I take orders. I don't make private deals. Joe made private deals. He had his way and I got my way. So go tell your committee you couldn't even get into the place.'

The door started to shut and then opened again. 'And don't hang around, Mack, and don't knock on the door any more or somebody comes out and reasons with you.' The door banged shut.

Sam did not leave the Market Street area until almost ten at night. It was always so effortlessly accomplished in the movies. Sinister types were always available to the hero. He hit the roughest-looking bars he could find. He'd never been adept at striking up a conversation with a stranger. He tried to select suitable-looking types and start a conversation and steer it around to the point where he could state his problem in a hypothetical way. Now just suppose, for the sake of argument, this friend of mine wanted to pay to get the man who is messing around with his wife beaten up.

'The chump better get a couple friends and take care of it himself. Or let him have the wife. He'll be better off without her.'

One man looked properly violent and comfortably shrewd. But after the question was stated, the man said, 'Let your friend turn the other cheek and ask God for forgiveness for plotting evil. Let him get down on his knees and pray for the seducer to see the sinfulness of his ways and the wanton woman to find her way back to Christ.'

Discouraged, he tried another tack. Who runs the

town? Who is the big wheel of the New Essex underworld?

A sad-faced bartender gave him a low-key lecture on that subject. 'Chief, you better stay away from that television set. As far as rackets, this town is out to lunch. Nothing is organized and I hope to God it never is. There's a couple of floating games, and there's some girls to be found, and once in a while a tea peddler comes through, and then there's the union strongarm stuff now and then. But there's no boss because there's no control of the wards. That's where the rackets get a good hold. If you can deliver a block vote, you can hire the politicians to keep the cops off your neck and then you can consolidate. All around here is small timey, Chief.'

'How about a man like, say, Joe Tanelli?'

'I don't like badmouthing the dead, but Joe was a nothing. He'd do a little fencing when there wasn't any risk. And he'd bank a game now and then. He was just smart enough to know he couldn't expand or somebody would step on him. We got tough, smart cops here, Chief.'

'So who is more important than Joe was?'

'I'm trying to tell ya and you don't hear me or something. I'm not getting through. There are maybe three or four Joe Tanellis. Boys working the angles. A good week maybe they make three bills. What you're talking about doesn't happen here. This town has the lid on. I hope it's for keeps. A long time ago I got tired of wondering when I was going to get worked over for selling the wrong brand of beer. That's why I moved here.'

Sam knew from the way his mouth felt that he was getting slightly drunk. 'I'll tell you what I really want.'

'Let me tell you something first. I don't want to hear it. I don't want to know nothing about what you've got to buy or sell. The less I know, the better I sleep at night.'

'But—'

'Let's be friends. Here's one on the house. Now, you want to keep talking, we talk women or baseball. Take your choice.'

He drove carefully back to Harper and directly to the Kimballs' party. It was out in their yard behind their house. Dorrie Kimball found him a cold piece of steak and heated it over what was left of the charcoal embers. It was leathery. There were a dozen couples. They were playing an intricate game that amused them vastly and left him spectacularly cold. When he had a chance he got Carol over into the shadows.

'I was a great success,' he said bitterly. 'I was overwhelmed by my own competence. It was like trying to sell dirty post cards at a Sunday-school wienie roast.'

'How much have you had to drink?'

'Plenty. It was an occupational hazard. I skulked through low dives, my collar turned up, my thumb on the button of my switch-blade knife. I've been called Doc, Mack and Chief. Oh, the hell with it!'

'Can you do *anything*?'

'I can call Sievers Monday morning. My God, this is a horrible party!'

'Ssh, darling. Not so loud. And it isn't *that* bad.'

'How soon can we leave?'

'I'll give the usual signal when we can. What a ghastly piece of luck, Mr. Tanelli dying like that!'

The drink Joe Kimball had given him seemed to be having more effect than all the others he had had. He swayed and peered down at her. 'Ghastly luck for good old Joe, too.'

'Don't be nasty to me.'

'I've got it figured out. You know what it is, don't you? It's the finger of fate diddling little Sammy Bowden. That good man. That noble and righteous man. Ah, how he's slipped! Now he goes forth to hire assassins. But we can't make it easy for him. Because then ole Sam will not be sufficiently aware of his fall from perfect grace. We gotta make him roll in it. We have to impress it on him so he won't forget it.'

'Darling, please.'

'Law and Order Bowden, we all called him around the office. The next best thing to the second coming. His strength was as the strength of ten because his grail was full. The brittle type. He could break but not bend. He would never compromise with his honor. And what a pitiful sight he is these days. Slinking through the slums, picking pockets, drinking canned heat, bumming dimes. They say that any day now he's going to be arrested for indecent exposure.'

The crack of her small hard palm against his cheek was loud and shocking. The sting made his eyes water. He looked down at her and she did not look angry or hurt. She stared up at him quite calmly.

'Hey!' he said.

'Drinks or no drinks, I don't think it is an awfully good time for us to start feeling sorry for ourselves, dear.'

'But I was just—'

'Mad at yourself for not being able to do something entirely out of your line and contrary to what you believe in. So you were starting to roll in bathos, rubbing it in your hair.'

'That's a sneaky right you've got there, pardner.'

'Well, were you?'

'I guess.'

‘I need a lot of strength to lean on at this point. Up until a few minutes ago there’s been plenty.’

‘It’s back now. Resume leaning.’

‘Are you mad at me?’

‘Enraged, furious and plotting revenge,’ he said, and kissed the tip of her nose.

To his astonishment she began to cry, thoroughly and helplessly. When she had begun to quiet down he learned the reason for the tears. It had upset her to strike him. All our emotional reactions are becoming shrill and raggedy, he thought. Tension is washing the sand from under our castle walls.

On Monday morning the local branch of Apex gave him the information he needed in order to phone Sievers in California. Mr. Sievers was not in the office, but he would call back. It was eleven before Sam could place his first call because of the time differential, and three before Sievers returned the call.

Though the connection was clear, Sievers had a sound of remoteness, of lack of interest.

‘Heart attack? That’s too bad.’

‘It makes it pretty awkward for me, Sievers.’

‘I can see how it would.’

‘Who shall I contact for the same … kind of service?’

‘I don’t think there’s anybody else to go to.’

‘What do I do?’

‘It might be set up some other place. Some people might be sent in. It would cost more and it would take some time.’

‘Can you help me with it?’

‘I’m pretty well snowed under out here. And … frankly, I’m on a different basis here, Bowden. I mean that was a personal arrangement. I can't do anything officially. Not along that sort of line. Do you understand?'

'I think so.'

'I did what I could. You had a bad break.'

'Maybe I can find somebody on my own.'

'I don't think you can. And it would be a bad risk. You might better just … get your people out of the way.'

'I … I see.'

'Sorry I can't be more helpful.'

It was a most unsatisfactory conversation. And it meant the end of a possible line of defense. They would have to fall back to another defensive position.

He talked it over on Monday night with Carol. She took it more calmly than he had anticipated.

'I know that it makes a certain kind of sense,' she said, 'but we will be so dispersed. Nance and Jamie down at camp. Bucky and me off God knows where. It leaves only you and that frightens me, darling. What good will any of us be if something should happen to you?'

'I'm going to be the most devout coward you ever heard of, honey. I'll take room at the New Essex House and I won't go out after dark, and I won't open the door unless I know damn well for sure who has knocked.'

'And then suppose nothing happens? When do we come back? When do we know it's over?'

'I don't think he's going to be very patient when he gets out. I think he'll make a move and I think he'll make it at me, and I'm going to make certain it will be unsuccessful, and if he does, then we'll have the evidence that will send him back for a long time.'

'Oh, yes. For a year, or three years, and then we can have such a fine time planning just what we'll do when they let him out again. It will be just like this month has been. Full of nervous smiles and bad jokes.'

'It will work out.'

'Please forgive me for asking you if it would be possible for you to stop saying that to me. It makes me feel as if you're patting me on the head. We hope it will work out. We very truly much hope so. But there aren't any written guarantees, are there, darling?'

'No. We can only do everything we can. And along that line, you will be charmed to learn that tomorrow I am becoming a dashing and dangerous figure, with the help of Captain Dutton.'

'What do you mean?'

'He is arranging the permit for me. He wasn't as reluctant as I expected him to be. At lunchtime I go pick up a very ugly and efficient device manufactured by Smith and Wesson. And when the harness is properly fitted, it will hang right here. It will nestle in a thing called a spring-clip holster. Nobody can snatch it away, but when I reach for it properly it will, Dutton claims, jump right into my hand. Then all I'll need will be a case of gin, a great big willing blonde and a shabbly little private office.'

She looked at him in a level way. 'So many gay little jokes. And such a wide, glassy, self-conscious smile.'

'What the hell do you want me to do? Clench my teeth and look steely-eyed? Of course I'm self-conscious about it! It isn't exactly my line, you know. I'm scared of Cady. I'm scared the way a kid having a nightmare is scared. The thought of him makes my hands sweat and makes my belly feel hollow. I'm so scared I'm going to wear that gun and tomorrow night I'm going to take so many cartridges up on the hill that by the time I'm through I'm going to be able to draw and fire and hit what I aim at. I'm going to feel like a little boy playing cops and robbers. I'm going to feel self-conscious. And so I'll make my forlorn little quips out of pure nervousness. But it's going to be a lot more comfortable to be a target that can shoot back.'

He stopped his pacing and looked at her and saw the quiet tears rolling down her cheeks. He sat beside her and took her in his arms and kissed the salty eyes.

'I shouldn't bellow at you,' he mumured.

'I … shouldn't have said what I did. I just got tired … of the frantic gaiety we coat everything with. It's gotten to be a nervous habit, but I guess it's the way we are.' She smiled wanly at him. 'And I couldn't stand a ponderous, humorless husband. I … I'm glad you're getting the gun. I'll feel better, really.'

'Me, my gun, and my asinine chatter.'

'I take all three. And gladly.'

'Now, then. Back to scheduling. We leave early Friday morning. We find a place for you and Bucky. We stay there Friday night. Saturday we see the birthday girl. I stay with you Saturday night at the place we find, and Sunday I drive back into town and—'

'Why don't we take both cars, dear? When we go to camp we can leave the MG at the place where I'm going to stay, and then on Sunday you can drive it back to the city when you check into the hotel.'

'Good deal.'

'I'm going to hate being away from you.'

'You are not alone.'

He wore the short-barreled revolver home on Tuesday night. The harness chafed him, and he realized it would be a long time before he could become accustomed to it. He had worn it when he went back to the office, feeling vastly foolish, and suspecting that everyone who glanced at him on the street saw the suspicious bulge under his left arm.

He stood inspection while Carol circled him. Finally she said, 'I know it's there so I can see the sort of lump it makes, but actually, darling, I guess you're the type. You're thin and you like your jackets cut loosely anyway.'

'So this dish saunters in and I can see right away nobody ever has to tell her the time of day. She makes a production out of sitting down and crossing her gorgeous legs, and then she dives down into a pocketbook as big as a phone booth for midgets and comes up with a wad of green stuff that would gag a hippo. Then she leans over and starts counting out hundred-dollar bills on the corner of my desk. I was so busy counting with her I didn't even take time to look down the front of her dress.'

Carol struck a faintly bawdy pose and said, out of the corner of her mouth, 'What did the floozy want, baby?'

'Ah, after all the production, it was routine. She wanted me to kill a guy.'

'You gonna do it?'

'Tomorrow. After lunch. The joker needs killing. You see, tootsie, I got this mission. I go around killing the bad guys. The guys that got connections so the law can't touch them, see. I'm cleaning out the filth, see. I eliminate 'em, like those knight guys used to get rid of the dragons they had hanging around with blazing halitosis. I get paid for it and the big blondes are always grateful. Real grateful.'

'And that leer, my friend, is almost too convincing.'

'Trudge up the hill after a while and watch me show off after I get used to this thing. Dutton says don't aim it. Point it as naturally as you point your finger. Where's the Buck? I don't want him galloping into the line of fire.'

'Liz Turner took a whole swarm of kids to the County Fair.'

'A brave and noble lady.'

He went up to the range with three boxes of shells, and a piece of sheeting and some twine. He tied the sheeting around a tree thick enough to simulate a man's torso. He penciled a crude heart on the left side of the chest. At first he was discouragingly slow, awkward and inaccurate. The weapon had a flat, gutty bark, much more authoritative than the snapping of the twenty-two. He fired a couple of dozen rounds for accuracy, and then went back to the routine of drawing and firing, improving doggedly.

Carol came up the hill and said, 'You sound like a South American revolution, darling.'

'This is trickier than I thought.'

'Should you be so close?'

'It's a measured twenty feet, honey. This thing isn't designed for potting at long range. I don't know as I'm ready to show off; but I'll try.' He loosened the riddled sheet and turned it around to the fresh side and refastened it.

'What's that?'

'It's a heart.'

'It's too small and it should be more in the middle.'

'Stop bossing the job. Okay. I'm in position. And I'm half turned away from it. Hands at my sides. Casual and relaxed. When you happen to feel like it, yell "go."'

'Go!'

He caught the grip cleanly, found the trigger as he wheeled, and emptied the cylinder. He put five black holes in the target, the first one in the abdominal area, one at the waist, and three fairly well centered in the chest.

'Wow!' she said, genuinely awed. 'Did one miss?'

'No. You keep the hammer on an empty chamber. You fire the first one double action.'

She looked slightly pale and her throat worked as she swallowed. 'Maybe my imagination is a little too vivid, darling. But it seems … so horribly functional.'

'It's completely functional. It's designed to be used on people. It's designed for maximum speed and maximum killing power for its size. There's nothing pretty about it, or romantic about it.'

He broke the gun and ejected the cases and reloaded. 'Want to try it?'

'I don't think so. I think I'd rather not.'

'Does the demonstration make you feel any better?'

She nodded. 'It does, Sam. It really does. But it's funny to think of you … I mean …'

'I know just what you mean. Lovable, mild old Sam. Dutton knows it too. And he very carefully made his point, in a roundabout way. He told me the armed forces had a lot of trouble in World War Two and in Korea with boys who would not fire their weapons. They are not certain of the basic cause. Something to do with civilization, Christian upbringing, respect for the life and dignity of the individual. He said that they get them on the cops. They'll get a rugged kid with good reflexes who does just fine on the target range. And then he'll get in a tight spot. He'll do exactly as he's been taught, right up to the point of aiming, and with his finger on the trigger. And he will stop right there, and if it is the wrong situation, they'll have a dead cop. I don't know about myself. I can really kill hell out of that tree, lips drawn back in a killer's sneer.

But if it was flesh and blood? I don't know. *I don't really know.* If I'd had any combat I would know. I think I could. I've got to make this so automatic with me that pulling the trigger is a part of the total action, and not a separate piece at the end. Then if I can start, I can go through it all the way. I hope.'

She tilted her head and studied him. 'There isn't much pretense about you, Sam. I mean you take such long, cold looks at yourself.'

'If you mean I don't consider myself a dashing figure, you're right. I am a sedentary, forty-year-old office worker, with a mortgage, a family and an insurance program. I am suited to this new aroma of violence and menace in the same way that George Gobel would feel at home as a Golden Gloves contestant in the heavyweight classification. It is a triteness to say that life makes curious and unexpected demands on you. I'm trying to face this one, but, my Indian maiden, there's something about it that makes me feel like a white mouse in a snake pit.'

She came up to him and held his wrists. 'And I tell you, you are not a white mouse. You are as brave as any man. You have warmth and strength. You know how to love and be loved. This is a great and rare art. You are my man, and I wouldn't want you changed in any way.'

He kissed her and then stood holding her in his arms. He looked down over her shoulder, and the dark gleam of the sun in his right hand looked incongruous. He was holding his wrist canted so that the weapon would not touch her pale-blue blouse. And beyond the gun he could see the white target and the penciled heart and five black holes.

CHAPTER EIGHT

On Friday they left early and drove southeast toward the pleasant little vacation villages in the lake area. Bucky seemed willing to accept the idea that Carol wanted a vacation from doing all the housework and he could come along too. It was, they told him, the next best thing to going away to camp.

They drove slowly and took side roads and arrived at the town of Suffern, ninety miles from Harper, at lunchtime. They had a good lunch in the quiet dining room of a lakeside inn called The West Wind. It was an old-fashioned frame building, with the tall and awkward dignity of the Victorian period. A busy little cricket of a man showed them two third-floor rooms on the lakeside with connecting bath. The weekly rate was reasonable and the rooms, with maple furniture and rag rugs, were clean and cheery. The rate included breakfasts and dinners, the use of the tiny beach, the hotel rowboats when available, the English croquet court, and the two tennis courts.

Yes, there were other children in the hotel, and they had never made it a policy to exclude children, but no pets, please. Even the oblique mention of Marilyn visibly saddened Bucky. It was not at all necessary, Sam decided, to use a different name. It would be theatrical, ludicrous and unnecessary. Carol said she would write directly to the office and, as an additional precaution, use envelopes not marked with the return address of The West Wind.

After Carol and Bucky had unpacked and changed, they went for a walk through the village, and then came back and waited until the croquet court was free. Carol was grimly accurate, and took high glee in whacking Sam's ball off into the hinterlands whenever she could get near enough to hit it. Sam teamed up with Bucky, but she still won readily.

That night, after they were in the big double bed, Carol said, 'I'm going to be terribly extravagant and buy a tennis racket. I'm terribly flabby. I need to tighten up.'

'Flabby? Flabby? Where? Here? Or possibly here?'

'*Stop* it, you darn fool.'

'Do you think you'll be happy here?'

'Not happy, darling. But as contented as I could be anywhere away from you.' Suddenly she giggled.

'What is it?'

'Bucky. His lordly disgust when those two little girls made their overtures.'

'I noticed he joined the fun and games nevertheless.'

'But in a superior and patronizing way. He's such a male little male.'

'And tomorrow the birthday girl.'

'Fifteen. Gosh, that's a terrible year.'

'Heresy.'

'No, it isn't. I was desperately unhappy at fifteen. Every mirror broke my heart. I was a mess. And so I wasn't going to be able to marry him.'

'Who was he?'

'Don't snicker at me now. Clark Gable. I had it all arranged. He was going to come to Texas to make a movie, and it was going to be a movie about oil wells. And I was going to go out to where they were making the movie and one day he would turn and he would look right at me, and smile in that funny quizzical way, with one eyebrow up and one down, and he'd stop the cameras and come over and look at me. Then he would signal to somebody, who would come running to him and he would say, pointing at me as I stood proud and haughty in my beauty, "She is my next leading lady. Fix up the contracts." But, oh dear, I was such a mess.'

'I had an intense and disturbing affair with Sylvia Sidney. She'd curl up in my arms like a silky little kitten and tell me it really didn't matter at all to her that I was nearly twenty pounds overweight. Now who's snickering?'

'I'm sorry, honey.'

'Then, of course, there was my Joan Bennett phase. And Ida Lupine for a time. And Jean Harlow. Jean used to drive out from Paris and wait for me in her Pierce-Arrow convertible behind the hangar. After I landed my riddled aircraft, gun barrels still smoking, and three more Huns to my credit, I would saunter, lean and casual and deadly, back to the big car. My incredible luck was due to her black-mesh stocking I tied to my upper arm before every combat operation. She used to bring out a hamper of iced champagne and that night they would see us in all the gay places of Paris, the undulant platinum blonde and the tall veteran pilot with that look of far places in his eyes and great and humble bravery.'

'Really?'

'She left me for a British major. On my very next assignment, I forgot the stocking. A German ace pounced on me out of the clouds. As I went down in flames, I saluted him and he waggled his wings out of courtesy to a dying hero.'

'Heavens to Betsy!'

'That's a very insulting snicker. It's a sort of sniggling sound.'

'Gosh, I wish it could be like this. I mean so safe. And all of us together. I don't want Sunday to come and I don't want to stand out there making my mouth smile while you drive away.'

'Don't think about it.'

'I can't stop.'

'Perhaps you could be distracted.'

'M—mmm. Perhaps.'

As had been prearranged by letter, they picked Jamie up at his camp before lunch. He was brown and thin and scrubbed to a startling state of cleanliness. Then they drove three miles along the lake shore road to Minnatalla to get Nancy. Nancy looked overwhelmingly healthy, and she had stars in her eyes.

They drove thirty miles due east to the small city of Aldermont for a festive meal in the dining room of the Hotel Aldermont. The hostess gave them an alcove of the dining room where they had more privacy.

Nancy was bubbling over. The camp was wonderful this year. Mr. Teller was pretty creepy, but he kept out of the way. She was assistant chairman of the social committee, and Tommy Kent was chairman of the Gannatalla social committee, so they had meetings often to make arrangements. Tommy was doing wonderfully. Mr. Menard had made Tommy a sort of personal assistant. One redheaded girl got poison ivy so badly she had to be sent home. Another girl fell off a horse and sprained her shoulder, but she wasn't going home. There was a new fast boat for the water skiing, and the camps took turns with it. Tommy was the regular driver.

When Nancy had run down, Jamie gave a sketchy account of his adventures. There was a wise guy in his cabin, and so Jamie had put the gloves on with him and Mr. Menard stopped the fight after Jamie had knocked the other boy down twice and now they were friends. He'd passed his junior lifesaving. He had killed a snake with a stick. He was making his own bow for archery. Out of lemon wood. You had to scrape it with pieces of glass, and you made your own cord out of winding linen thread and then rubbing beeswax on it.

After lunch Sam went out and got the presents out of the car. Nancy was delighted with everything. There were the traditional small consolation presents, one apiece for Jamie and Bucky. Consolation for it being somebody else's birthday.

Carol, by arrangement, took Bucky off and left Sam at the table with Nancy and Jamie so he could tell them about the new arrangement. They could know their mother and Bucky were at The West Wind in Suffern, but they were to keep it to themselves. Nancy asked if she could tell Tommy, and Sam told her she could. In the event of serious emergency they could phone their mother in Suffern, and phone him either at the office or the New Essex House.

Jamie looked somberly at his father and said, 'It's just like running away, isn't it?'

'You hush!' Nancy said.

'Never mind, Nance. Yes, son. In a sense it is. But I'm not hiding. I'm going to be careful, but I'm not going to hide. They put women and children in the lifeboats first.'

'Tommy and Mr. Menard keep telling me to stay with the other kids all the time,' Jamie said. 'I wish that dirty prisoner would come to camp. We'd fix him, boy. We'll all get stones and we'll all throw at once. Those stones'll plunk him right in the head. Then we'll tie him up and take him in the kitchen and run him through the brand-new meat slicer that cost a hundred and twenty bucks, Mr. Menard said.'

'Jamie!' Nancy said. 'Don't say such terrible things.'

'Now she's fifteen does she get to give me orders?' Jamie demanded.

'When you come up with an idea guaranteed to spoil her lunch, she has a right to object.'

'And I'll set it to slice him real thin,' Jamie said darkly.

'I too think that is enough of that line of speculation, young man. You kids have the picture now. Don't either of you get careless. The man has a car. He's out of jail. When he finds the house closed, he can easily find out in the village where you kids go in the summer. I know he knows Nancy by sight, and I'd guess he knows you by sight too. Ready to go? Your mother and Bucky will be out in the lobby.'

'It's funny to think about nobody being home,' Nancy said. She touched her father's arm shyly as they stood up. 'Will you please be real careful, Daddy.'

'I will.'

On Sunday night Sam had dinner in the grill room at the New Essex House by himself, and then went into the bar for a nightcap before going up to bed. He stood at the bar and nursed his drink and felt very alone in the world. At the end of the drive that went up to the side entrance of The West Wind, he had stopped and looked back and waved. Carol and Bucky, standing close together on the green grass of the lawn, waved back. He drove the little car too fast all the way back to New Essex.

A booming voice in his ear startled him. 'Out on the town, Sam?'

He turned and looked into the wide, smiling face of Georgie Felton, and tried to register enough pleasure to avoid rudeness.

Georgie Felton was a real-estate broker and a highly successful one. He was a large and solid fat man, of heavy-handed humor and an impenetrable hide. He treated women with an overwhelming air of courtly gallantry, which, by the time of the second meeting, became curiously spiced with rather coarse innuendo. With men he was the traditional jolly boy. He belonged to a staggering number of civic and service organizations. In the background was a round Angela Felton and four small round Feltons. He would be called Georgie until the day he died. Carol could not stand him. She could not understand how he could be successful. When they were house hunting he had taken her to see houses so remarkably unsuitable that she suspected he was making an obscure joke. But Georgie was very serious.

'Hello, Georgie.'

Georgie clapped him on the right shoulder and said, 'Benny, get Mr. Bowden another of whatever he's having.'

'No, really.'

'Come on. If you're still on your feet, you can handle another one. What brings you into town tonight? Big date with a mysterious blonde?'

'I'm staying here the hotel.'

Georgie's eyebrows went up. 'Oh, ho! Sam, old buddy, it happens to the best of us. You can't get along with 'em and you can't get along without 'em. One little wrong word and there you are. Doghoused.'

Sam felt intense irritation, He certainly had no intention of telling Georgie his troubles, 'It isn't like that, Georgie. Two of the kids are at camp, and so we closed the house and Carol is taking a little vacation with our youngest.'

Georgie nodded in a sage way. 'You hear a lot about that, Sam. A marital vacation. Get out of each other's hair for a while.' He gave Sam a lecherous wink and elbowed him so hard in the ribs he knocked him off balance. 'But I've never been able to talk Angie into it. Teach me how to arrange it, Sammy boy.' And he threw his head back and laughed. He nudged Sam again. 'You got something lined up yet, old buddy? Want to borrow Uncle Georgie's little black book?'

'No, thanks, Georgie.'

Sam blocked the next nudge. 'You got in the wrong business, Sammy boy. I'll tell you, there's something about walking through a nice new house that brings out the best in a pretty little woman. You'd be surprised at some of the ones I run into, laddy.'

'For God's sake, Georgie, stop ramming that elbow into me.'

'What? Well, parm me all over the place. I guess it's one of those habits. Now there's some stuff right over there against the wall. That off-the-shoulder deal. You like that?'

'It's nice. And the man with her has shoulders on him.'

'Let's you and me go to a real live place. It's dead in here.'

'I'm sorry, Georgie. I'm going to go up and read awhile and go to bed.'

'Aw, come on, pal. We could …' Georgie stopped abruptly. Sam looked down at him. Georgie was moistening his lips and looking down into the front of Sam's suit coat. Sam looked down and saw the butt grip of the gun. He fixed his coat quickly to hide it.

'What the hell are you carrying that thing for?' Georgie asked in a beefy whisper. His expression was shocked.

'It's like this, Georgie. There's a man gunning for me. He might show up any time.'

Georgie looked around nervously. 'You're kidding.'

Sam looked at him solemnly. 'We lawyers make enemies, Georgie.'

'Is … the man in town?'

'He might come through that door any minute.'

Georgie edged back. 'Well, I'll be go to hell.'

'Don't talk about it to anyone, Georgie.'

'No. No, I sure won't.' He looked at his wristwatch. 'I'll be running along. Nice to run into you, Sam.' He was backing away as he spoke.

Sam's pleasure in the incident faded quickly. Georgie would talk. Georgie would tell everyone he ran into. He finished the unwanted drink and went up to bed.

Nothing happened on Monday or Tuesday or Wednesday. Sam followed his cautious routine. He called Carol twice from the office. She had a determined cheerfulness plastered over her tension and her loneliness. But the camouflage was imperfect. On Wednesday morning there was a long, chatty letter from her. She described the other tenants in the hotel. She had found a tennis partner, a rangy, powerful girl whose husband was a Marine captain on overseas duty. Her game was rusty but it was beginning to come back. Bucky had shown such an interest she had found him a small racket and she was teaching him the basic strokes. He was learning quite quickly. Bucky was contemptuous of the poor television reception in the lounge. There was a good loan library in the big drugstore in the town. And she missed him. They both missed him and missed the house and missed the campers.

On Thursday afternoon he decided that he had had enough of waiting and wondering. It was time the white mouse ventured out of the hole and found where the cat was.

He arrived at Nicholson's Bar on Market Street at six o'clock. The bar part was a narrow room with striated plywood walls painted dark green, with bar stools and the edge of the bar upholstered in green imitation leather. There were mirrors and chrome and tricky lighting on the back bar. It had a scuffed, worn look. The plastics and paint were not holding up well. The mirrors and the chrome were peeling. The television over the bar was on and there was an out-of-order sign on the jukebox. There were three men sitting at the far end of the bar, heads close together, talking in low, important voices. There were no other customers at the bar.

Beyond the bar part was a wider room, a cocktail lounge. The daylight did not reach back to that room. Two amber spots were angled at a small, empty platform which held a midget white piano and a very battered set of drums. In the reflected glow he could see two couples at two tables in the lounge. A waitress leaned against the frame of the wide doorway between the bar and the lounge. She wore a dark-green uniform and a soiled white apron. She was a washed-out, sandy blonde and she was picking at a back molar with her thumbnail.

The bartender stood endlessly polishing a glass and watching the television screen. Sam took a stool on the curve of the bar near the door, then, feeling self-conscious, he moved to the end stool around the curve where, by sitting sideways, his back was to the wall and he could see the door.

The bartender drifted over to him, looking at the screen until the last possible moment. He wiped the bar in front of Sam and said, 'Yes, sir?'

'Miller, I guess.'

'Coming up.'

He brought the beer and a glass, picked up Sam's dollar, rang it up, put a half dollar and a nickel on the bar.

'Pretty slow?'

'Always is, this time of day. We do a late business.'

'Has Max been in lately?'

He saw the bartender look him over more carefully. 'What Max do you mean? We got a lot of Maxes.'

'The bald one with the tan.'

The bartender pulled at his underlip. 'Oh, *that* Max. I seen him one time lately. Let me think. Sure, it was last Saturday night. He was in, oh, maybe ten minutes. Two fast shots and gone. He had some trouble, you know. He slugged a cop and they put him in city jail for thirty days.'

'How about Bessie McGowan? She been in?'

'She's always in. I wish to hell she'd pick another spot for a change. If you know her, you know how she gets. She ought to be coming in any time now.'

One of the men at the other end of the bar called him and the bartender walked away. Ten minutes later, when Sam was thinking of signaling for another beer, a woman walked in. She could not have selected anything to wear which could have made her look more grotesque. She had on white pumps with four-inch heels, skintight black bullfighter pants, a wide white leather belt with a gilt buckle, a tight sweater-blouse in a red-and-white horizontal candy stripe. A woman with a perfect figure might have been able to carry it off with a certain amount of theatrical success. But this was a woman in her middle years, with a mop of hair so abused by dyes that it was the color and texture of sun-bleached hemp. She had a puffy chipmunk face, square red lips painted boldly on. Her waist was surprisingly narrow in contrast to the wobbling massiveness of hip, the vast and doughy contours of the barely credible breasts. It was alarmingly obvious that she wore nothing under pants and blouse except an uplift bra that staunchly focused and aimed the great breasts dead ahead like fire-control direction on a battleship. She walked in an almost visible cloud of musky perfume, and she dangled a white shoulder bag from a single finger, so that it nearly dragged on the floor. She was grotesque, ludicrous and incredible. Yet there was nothing pathetic about her. She was carrying on her own gallant war against time in her own way. She was in the great bawdy tradition of the mining camps and the frontiers.

She plopped the white bag on the center of the bar and, in a voice worn by tobacco, whisky and long use into a texture that was like a stage whisper by a baritone, said, 'Jolt and water, Nick.'

'The check come?' the bartender asked warily.

'Yes, yes, the check came. The check came. Here you go, you suspicious louse. Hit me with the grandpa today.' She slapped a five-dollar bill on the bar.

As he reached for the bottle the bartender said, motioning toward Sam, 'Friend of yours asking after you, Bessie.'

She turned and stared at him and then walked over to him. Up close she gave that curious larger-than-life impression that accomplished actresses know how to project. He saw that her eyes were large and gray and exceptionally lovely.

'My Gawd, a man who stands up. Sit down, old friend, before I die of shock.' She sat on the stool next to him, and studied him, puzzled. 'Honest, I got to watch these blackouts. Usually I can come up with a clue. But I draw a big blank. Clue me, Louie.'

The bartender put the shot glass of whisky, a glass of water and her change in front of her.

'Well over a month ago, Bessie. You were out at one of the joints on the shore east of town. With a bald man named Max. You told me this was your favorite spot.'

'It's going to stop being anybody's favorite spot if Nick and Whitey keep on being so damn chintzy about money all the time. I remember that Max. So I was with him. It figures. But what the hell were we doing talking to you?'

'What do you mean?'

'You've got a haircut and clean fingernails and a press in your suit, mister. You talk like your folks sent you to college. You could be a doctor or a dentist. Max would talk to bums. Nobody but bums. You gentlemen types made him ugly.'

'So since you recommended the place, I thought I'd stop and get a drink.'

'So you thought you'd stop and get drink.'

She looked at him with a compelling and horrible coquetry.

He gingerly moved his arm to get it away from the pressure of a giant breast and said quickly, 'Seen Max around lately?'

'No, thanks. He was in jail. I guess he's out now. I like my fun. Christ, everybody knows me knows that. I got a little income and I get along. I'm what you call friendly.

I've seen a lot of people, and I've been a lot of places. And I can put up with a lot. Who's perfect? But let me tell you about that Max Cady. He's all man. I got to give him that. But he's mean as a snake. He doesn't give a damn for anybody in the world but Max Cady. You know what he did to me?' She lowered her voice and her face hardened. 'We were in my place. I'm curious about him. You know. You want to know about people. So I'd been asking him and all I get is the brush. So there we are and I fix him a drink and I say, "Let's stop the runaround, Maxie. Fill me in. Brief me. What's with you? Tell Mama."'

She knocked off the shot, took a sip of water, and yelled at Nick for a refill. 'What does he do? He beats up on me. On me! Bessie McGowan. Right in my own place, drinking my liquor, he gets up out of one of my chairs and he thumps me all over the place. And grinning at me all the time. Let me tell you, the way he was going at it, I thought he was going to kill me, honest. And then all the lights went out.

'At dawn I wake up. I was on the floor, and I was a mess. He was gone. I crawled to bed on my hands and knees. When I got up again, I got to a mirror. I had a face on me like a blue basketball. I was so sore all over I couldn't move without yelping. I got the doc over and told him I fell downstairs. I've never yelled cop in my life, but I was close. Three cracked ribs. Forty-three bucks dental. I looked so awful it was a week before I stirred out of the place, and even then I was walking like an old lady. It's a good thing I'm strong as a horse, mister. That go-round would have killed most women. And you know, I don't feel exactly right yet. When I read about his trouble, I sent out for a bottle and I drank it all myself. He isn't a human being. That Max is an animal. All I did was ask questions. All he had to do was say that he wanted me to shut up.'

She drank her second shot, and when she called Nick back he ordered another beer.

'So he's no friend of yours, Bessie.'

'If I saw him dead in the street, I'd buy drinks for the house.'

'He's no friend of mine.'

She shrugged. 'How do you mean, just seeing us that once?'

'I didn't. I made that up.'

The gray eyes turned very cold. 'I don't like gags.'

'My name is Sam Bowden.'

'So what's that got to do with ... Did you say Bowden?'

'Maybe he called me the lieutenant.'

'Yes, he did.'

'Bessie, I want you to help me, I don't know what to expect. He's going to try to hurt me. Somehow. I want to know if he gave you any clue.'

She kept her voice very low. 'He was a funny bugger, Sam. He didn't have too much to say. He didn't show you much of his insides. But twice he talked about Lieutenant Bowden. And both times it gave me the cold creepers, right up and down my back. Part the way he looked. He didn't say anything that made sense, though. One time he said you were an old Army buddy and to show you how much he liked you he was going to kill you six times. He said he was going to make you last. He was drinking and I tried to, you know, kinda laugh it off like telling him he wouldn't kill anybody for real.'

'What did he say?'

'Nothing. He just gave me a look and he didn't say any

more that time. Do you know what he meant? How can you kill anybody six times?'

He looked down into his beer glass. 'If a man had a wife, three kids and a dog.'

She tried to laugh. 'Nobody'd do that.'

'He started with the dog. He poisoned it.'

Her face turned chalky. 'Dear sweet Jesus!'

'What else did he say?'

'There was just the one other time he talked about you. He said something like by the time I get around to the lieutenant, I'll be doing him a favor. He'll be begging for it. That kind of fits in with the other, doesn't it?'

'Would you come with me to police headquarters and sign a statement about what you heard him say?'

She looked at him for ten seconds. It seemed a very long time. 'You happen to be snuggling up to a girl graduate of Dannemora, dearie.'

'Would you?'

'I'll tell you what, snooks. Take a letter to J. Edgar. Dear Ed. Me and the boys were just . . .'

'There's a girl fifteen, a boy eleven, a boy six.'

'You're breaking my heart, dearie. In the first place I've seen the inside of that place too many times already. In the second place they wouldn't listen to anything Bessie McGowan says. In the third place it's a cruel world and I'm sorry if you got problems, but that's the way the ball bounces.'

'I'll beg you to—'

'Hey Nick! It turns out I didn't know this bum after all. How come you let ladies get insulted in this joint?'

'You don't have to do that,' Sam said.

She got off the stool. 'That's where I am, snooks. Right where I was heading all my life. Right to the place where I don't have to do anything about anything.'

'Not so loud, Bessie,' Nick said.

She picked up all her change except a dime. She pushed it toward Nick. 'Have a ball, lover. I'm finding a better joint.'

She yanked the street door shut behind her. Nick picked up the dime and studied it thoughtfully. 'That there is a pistol, friend. How'd you drive her out? Maybe I can use it sometime.'

'I wouldn't know.'

Nick sighed. 'Once upon a time she was Miss Indiana. She showed me the clipping. I said I didn't know it was a state that long ago. She busted me right in the eye with a left hook. Well, come back and see us.'

He walked down to Jaekel Street. Number 211 was a square, three-story frame house painted brown with yellow trim. A window sign announced ROOM FOR RENT. An old man sat in a rocking chair on the narrow porch, his eyes closed. There were two holes in the screen door, one of them mended. Sam pushed the doorbell and heard it ring in the back of the house. There was a smell of mold and acid and cabbage and soiled bedding. There was a screaming quarrel going on upstairs. He could hear the deep sound of a man's voice, slow and oddly patient, and then a shrill tirade that would go on for a long time. He could pick out a word here and there. He could look into the hallway and see a narrow dark table with several letters on it and a lamp with a fringed shade.

A gaunt old woman came down the hallway toward him. Her stride was astonishingly heavy. She stood inside the screening and said, 'Yay-yuss?'

'Does Mr. Cady live here?'

'Nope.'

'Mr. Max Cady?'

'Nope.'

'But he did live here?'

'Yay-yuss. But he don't no more. I wouldn't take him back if he wanted. We want no truck with fighting and polices, Marvin and me. No part of it. No, sir. And jail folks. That's where he was. Jailed. Shut up tight. Come back Friday and got his stuff. I'd had Marvin put it in the cellar. He didn't want to pay me rent for parking space ahind the house, but I said as how I'd have the law right back on him in a minute and then he paid me and he drove his car off and that's the last of him.'

'Did he leave a forwarding address?'

'Now that would be downright stupid for a man never got any mail at all, wouldn't it?'

'Has anybody else come around asking for him?'

'You're the very first and I surely pray you're the last on account of Marvin and me, we don't cotton to folks like that.'

He phoned Dutton the next morning. Dutton said he would see if anybody could get a line on Cady.

Nothing happened on Friday. On Saturday he drove down to Suffern, and on Sunday they visited Nancy and Jamie. He was back at his desk on Monday morning. He had not told Carol about the story he got from Bessie McGowan. He did not want her to know he had gone down into Cady's area, nor did he wish to alarm her.

Nothing happened on Monday. Or Tuesday.

The phone call from Mr. Menard came through on Wednesday, at ten in the morning on the last day of July, the day when Carol was to have gone down and picked

Jamie up in the afternoon and taken him back to Suffern with her. It was his final day of camp.

When he realized who was calling, he felt as though his heart had stopped.

'Mr. Bowden? Jamie's been hurt, but it's not serious.'

'How was he hurt?'

'I think you'd better come down here if you can. He's on his way over to the Aldermont Hospital now, and it will probably be best if you go directly there. I repeat, it's not serious. He's not in danger. Sheriff Kantz will want to talk to you sooner or later. I had to … give him what information I had, of course.'

'I'll leave right away. Have you informed my wife?'

'She left before the call got through. I understand she's on her way here. I'll send her over to Aldermont and we could keep the little fellow here with us, if she agrees to that.'

'Tell her I think that would be a good idea. Where's Nancy?'

'On the way over with her brother and Tommy Kent.'

'Can you please tell me what happened to the boy?'

'He was shot, Mr. Bowden.'

'Shot!'

'It could have been more serious. Much more serious. It's on the inside of his upper left arm, about three inches above the elbow. It made an ugly gash. He lost blood, and, naturally, it scared him.'

'I would think so. I'll make it as quickly as I can.'

'Young Kent can give you the rest of the story at the hospital. Don't drive too fast, Mr. Bowden.'

CHAPTER NINE

Carol had been at the hospital for nearly an hour when Sam arrived at one-thirty. She and Nancy were in the semi-private room with Jamie when Sam walked in. Sam kissed her. She looked completely under control, but he felt the trembling of her mouth as he kissed her. Nancy had a subdued, troubled look. Jamie's face against the pillow was just pale enough under the tan to give him a greenish look. His left arm was bandaged, and he looked proud and excited.

'Hey, I didn't make a sound when they sewed it up, and I got six stitches.'

'Does it hurt?'

'Sort of, but not bad. Gosh, I can't wait to tell the kids at home. A real bullet. It hit my arm and went through the shed next to the mess hall, right in one side and out the other – zowie – and when they find it I can have it after the sheriff is through with it. I'd like it on one of those little wooden things under glass in my room.'

'Who did it?'

'Heck, who knows? That man, I guess. That Cady. A lot of the kids didn't even hear any shot. I didn't. I wish I'd heard it. He was a long way away, up on Shadow Hill someplace, the sheriff thinks.'

Sam began to understand the picture. 'Tell me about it, Jamie, from the beginning.'

Jamie looked uncomfortable. 'Well, I goofed up. I snitched Mr. Menard's shaving bomb and I was going to let Davey Johnstone have it right in the chops and then I was going to sneak it back. But I got caught. So I got ten days of doing pots, and this was the last day. Everybody hates pots. You got to use steel wool. I got ten whole days because it was sort of like stealing, even though it really wasn't. So you do the pots out by the shed. There's a faucet there, and, oh, this was about nine-thirty and I was doing the breakfast pots and I was nearly done almost.

'I was just standing there, sort of looking at the last one, and bam! I thought some joker had gone in the shed and hit it with something to scare me. Then my arm felt all hot and funny. I looked down and there was blood squirting out of it, squirting all over. I yelled as loud as I could and ran for Mr. Menard's cottage and other kids saw all the blood and they were running and yelling too, and they put a tourniquet on it. And then it all of a sudden started to hurt something terrible. And I cried, but not very much. By then Tommy went and got Nancy and then the sheriff came and we all rode over here in the sheriff's car about maybe a hundred miles an hour with the siren going. Boy, I wish I could do that again when my darn arm wasn't hurting.'

Sam turned to Carol. 'What happens now?'

'Dr. Beattie said he'd like to have him stay here overnight, and he should be all right to travel tomorrow. He gave him some whole blood.'

'There's going to be a scar,' Jamie said fervently. 'A real bullet scar. Will it hurt when it's going to rain?'

'I think you have to have the bullet in there, son.'

'Anyway, no other kid I know has a bullet scar.'

A smiling nurse came in and said, 'Time for this

wounded veteran to have his pink pill and a long nap.'

'Heck, I don't need any nap,'

'When can we see him again, Nurse?' Carol asked.

'At five, Mrs. Bowden.'

They walked to the stairs and went down to the hospital lobby. Carol, her face ghastly, turned toward Sam and said in a voice so low Nancy couldn't overhear, barely moving her bloodless lips, 'Now what? Now what? When does he kill one of them?'

'Please, honey.'

'Daddy, Sheriff Kantz is coming with Tommy,' Nancy said.

'Take your mother over to that couch and sit there with her, Nancy, please.'

The sheriff was a rangy man who wore boots and tan riding pants and a khaki shirt. He had an outdoor look about him, a gun belt, a wide-brimmed hat in his hand. He shook hands slowly, almost thoughtfully. His voice was nasal, with a tired sound about it.

'Guess we can talk over in that corner, Mr. Bowden. Sure, you sit in, Tommy.'

They pulled three chairs closer together. 'I'll tell you my end, Mr. Bowden, and then I'd like to ask you a couple questions. First off it looks like the range was about seven hundred yards. And down hill. Take a good rifle and a good scope and a knowledgeable man and it isn't a tough shot at all. I imagine if the wind wasn't cutting up too much, I could put nearly every shot in a circle about half again as big as a pie plate. If it were deer season, I'd have maybe a different idea about this. Your boy's arm was close to his side. The wind was a little gusty from the south. The boy was facing east. So it looks like one of those gusts drifted that slug over a few inches. Nobody was trying to scare the boy. They made a pretty good try at killing him. If he'd put his slug say two and a half inches further to his right, that boy would have been dead before he could fall all the way down.'

Sam swallowed hard and said, 'You don't have to—'

'I'm talking facts, Mr. Bowden. I'm not talking to see how much I can get you upset. And I wouldn't talk to your wife like this. If he'd hit the boy the way he wanted to, we'd have had us a real bad time trying to figure where the bullet came from. But he missed and he put two holes in the shack and that gave us a line of sight. It couldn't be direct, because the way the slug will drop, especially after going through a three-quarter-inch board. It put us on a line up the side of a knoll the kids call Shady Hill. There's a lot of back roads up in there and I know for a fact that there are plenty of places you can look down right into that camp. I've got a deputy named Ronnie Gideon I left working on it, and he's a good boy and he knows the woods and he can read track, and he'll find where the man with the gun was when he took aim. We were too late for any road block because we didn't know what to look for. I understand you can tell us who to look for, Mr. Bowden.'

'I can't prove he fired the shot. I can't prove he poisoned our dog. But I know it was Cady both times. Max Cady. He got out of federal prison last year in September, I think. He drives a gray Chevy sedan, about eight years old. You can phone Captain Mark Dutton in New Essex and he'll give you all you need to know on him.'

'He must have a pretty strong hate for you folks.'

'I was instrumental in getting him jailed for life. But they let him out after thirteen years. He was in for rape of a fourteen-year-old Australian girl during the war. He comes from bad stock. He's vicious and I think he's more than half demented.'

'Is he smart? Shrewd?'

'Yes.'

'Let's take a look at this situation now. Suppose he's picked up. He'll be miles from here. He won't have a rifle with him. He'll deny firing at any boy. Must have been a stray shot. He'll yell persecution. I don't know any good way to hold him, under the law.'

'That's just fine.'

'Now, you've got to think the way those people think. All right. This was carefully planned. He had to spend some time scouting the situation. So he had to think of what he was going to do after he killed the boy. He knew you'd point suspicion at him. So he'd have to either brazen it out, depending on no evidence showing up, or he'd have it all set so he could hide out. Killing a kid would attract a lot of attention. He couldn't be certain somebody didn't see him up on those back roads. So I'd say he's got a hole to hide in. He'll have it all stocked and he'll be in some out-of-the-way place where nobody will look for him.'

'You're so optimistic.'

'I'm trying to be practical. So you can know what to expect. I'll bet he's sore at himself for missing. I think he was planning to move fast and get out of the area. He may try to keep on moving fast. I'd say this is the time to be just as careful as you can possibly be.'

The sheriff stood up and smiled wearily. 'I'll get hold of the people up there in New Essex and then I'll put out a pick-up order on him. I think the thing to do would be to lock up you people.'

'I don't find that excruciatingly funny, Sheriff.'

'I can see how you wouldn't have much sense of humor left this afternoon.'

'What can I do, sir?' Tommy asked Sam.

'Could you go … No, I'll do that. I'll go over and pick up Bucky and bring him back here. Stay with the gals, Tommy.'

'All right, Mr. Bowden.'

'And thanks. Thanks a lot.'

It took him just a little over a half hour in the station wagon to reach camp. He found Sheriff Kantz with Mr. Menard in the administration cottage. The dull-looking young man with them was introduced as Deputy Ronnie Gideon.

Menard was obviously troubled. 'I don't know what we could have done to avoid this, Mr. Bowden.'

'I don't blame you in any way.'

'I am finding it very hard to accept the fact this was intentional. Sheriff Kantz assures me it is.'

The sheriff was tossing a small object into the air and catching it. 'This is the slug. Badly deformed. Thirty-caliber, I'd say. Mr. Menard here put a slew of kids to looking for it until they found it.'

'We're saying it was a stray bullet,' Menard said. 'Everybody is excited enough as it is. But I don't know what the parents are going to say when they get letters saying a stray bullet wounded a camper. I'm sorry, Mr. Bowden. I shouldn't be griping about my problems when yours are so much greater.'

'Did you find the place where the shot was fired from?' Sam asked.

The deputy nodded. 'Rock ledge. Prone position. About thirty feet from the road up there. He matted the moss on the rock. It was still springing back up. No car tracks, no empty cartridge case. Did find a chewed cigar butt. He'd rubbed it out on the rock. Mouth end still soggy.'

'If he'd killed the boy,' the sheriff said, 'we'd be sending it along to the lab to see if we could get a type on the saliva. But I don't see as how it does much good.'

'Cady smokes cigars.'

The sheriff looked blandly at Sam. 'Hope you got a permit for that thing you're carrying?'

'What? Oh, of course. Yes, I have a permit.'

'What do you plan to do now?'

'We were going to take Jamie out of camp today anyway. I think I'll go over to the girls' camp and get Nancy's gear and check her out.'

'And go home?'

'No. I'm going to leave my wife and children in the place where … she has been staying with the younger boy.'

'Any chance of this Cady knowing where that is?'

'I don't see how he could.'

The sheriff pursed his lips. 'Sounds okay to me. Leave them all there until he's picked up. But suppose he isn't picked up? How are you going to know when he gives up and goes away?'

'I guess we won't know.'

'Can't keep your family hid out forever.'

'I know that. I've thought of that. But what else can I do? Do you have any ideas?'

'The only one I got I'm not proud of, Mr. Bowden. Think of him like he's a tiger. You want to get him in out of the brush. So you stake out a goat and you hide in a tree.'

Sam stared at him. 'If you could possibly think I'd use my wife or any of my kids as bait for—'

'I told you I wasn't proud of it. You can guess what a tiger will do, I've heard, but you can't guess about a crazy man. He tried sniping this time. Next time he might try something else. I guess it's best to keep them hid. It's the best you can do.'

Sam looked at his watch. 'I'd like to collect Jamie's gear and pick up Bucky, Mr. Menard.'

'I've had his gear packed and brought up to the mess hall. Bucky is with my wife. I'll go get him. I'm sorry this was such a bad ending to Jamie's month.'

'I'm glad it wasn't worse.'

'We'll look forward to having him with us next year.'

Sam said goodbye to the sheriff and thanked him. The sheriff assured him there was a pretty good chance of Cady being picked up for questioning. But there was a hollow ring to his assurances.

Sam was back at the hospital by quarter to five. Nancy was very surprised when she found he had checked her out of camp, and disappointed she would have no chance to say goodbye, but she soon accepted it as a logical and inevitable decision.

She nodded slowly and said, 'I know. There's so many hills. I couldn't be outdoors anywhere in daylight without wondering if …' And she shuddered.

Sam phoned Bill Stetch from a booth in the hospital lobby and told him the situation and said he wouldn't be back in the office until Friday morning.

After they saw Jamie again and said good night to him, they had dinner at the Hotel Aldermont. Sam suggested to Carol that she drive on back to Suffern with

Nancy and Bucky and he would stay over and bring Jamie up the next day. But when he sensed how reluctant she was to be parted from him, he went to the hotel desk and took two rooms for the night. Tommy Kent tried to insist that he could get a bus back to camp, but Sam drove him back. Nancy had wanted to come along, but Sam told her to stay with her mother and Bucky. He was worried about Carol. She was entirely too reserved and subdued. During dinner she had joined in the conversation mechanically. She seemed far away from all of them.

As he drove the MG west toward the afterglow of the sunset, he said to his quiet passenger, 'Am I doing the right thing, Tommy?'

'Sir?'

'Try to put yourself in my shoes. What would you do?'

'I . . . I guess I'd do what you're doing.'

'You sound as if you have reservations.'

'It's not that, exactly, but it seems so . . . you know, waiting instead of doing anything.'

'Passive.'

'That's what I mean. But I can't think of anything you can do.'

'Society is well organized to protect me and my family from theft and arson and civil riot. The casual criminals are kept under reasonably good control. But it is not set up to deal with a man who is trying specifically and irrationally to kill us. I know I could put enough pressure to bear to get my family officially guarded around the clock. But it would merely give Cady pleasure in finding a way to outwit the guards. And if the police were pulled off, I could hire people as bodyguards. But that would be the same story, I'm afraid. And it would be a very artificial way to live. And it would be constant terror, especially since this has happened.'

'He won't be able to find out they're in Suffern?'

'Not unless he can manage to follow us when we leave Aldermont. But I don't think he's in this area any more. I think he is always a half step ahead of me. I think he knows damn well I would immediately pull both kids out of camp. I have the feeling he's back up near Harper. There's a lot of fairly wild country around there.'

'I sure wouldn't want anything to happen to Nancy.'

'Suffern doesn't sound as safe to me as it did before. I think I may move them again tomorrow.'

'I'd feel better about it, I think.'

Sam studied a road map for a long time before the two-car caravan started the hundred-mile trip from Aldermont north to Suffern. Jamie was in good spirits, and his color was back to normal. He had all the faintly patronizing nonchalance of a seasoned combat veteran. Carol was still peculiarly subdued and unresponsive. He led the way in the MG with Nancy, and Carol followed with the boys. He took a roundabout route over secondary roads, and after stopping twice to be certain they weren't followed, he continued with more confidence. It was a bright morning, with air so clear that every detail of far hills was sharp. The back roads went through beautiful country. It was the sort of day that raises the spirits. They were all together. He could be almost certain that Cady would be apprehended, and when that happened, maybe there would be some legal way he could be given tests to determine his sanity. Maybe some kind of pressure could be brought on Bessie McGowan to make her testify.

He looked frequently in the rearview mirror to see

how far behind Carol was. At approximately eleven o'clock, when they were forty miles south of Suffern, he glanced back at the precise moment when the station wagon made a wild swerve, swung back into a deep ditch and turned over. It seemed to happen in slow motion. He braked hard. Nancy looked back and screamed. He put the little car in reverse and shot backward and got out and ran to the car. He climbed up on the side of it and opened the door. Bucky was roaring with fright. He got Bucky out first and then Jamie and finally Carol. Nancy helped them down. There was no traffic. Sam made the three of them sit down in the thick grass at the top of the ditch near the fence.

Bucky had a lump like a half walnut on his forehead. Carol's mouth was bleeding. Jamie seemed unhurt. But Carol had gone to pieces. Completely. Her hysteria seemed more alarming to the children than the accident. He was unable to calm her. A small farm truck came rattling down the road. Sam ran out to hail it. A small, elderly, bitter-looking man was driving it. He looked directly ahead, jaw clamped shut, mouth working. Sam had to jump out of the way or be run down. He stood in the road, shaking with rage, yelling curses at the receding vehicle.

The next car stopped. It was a dusty sedan. The back was full of tools. Two big men in work clothes get out in a leisurely way and came over. Carol by that time had exhausted herself. She lay on her side, holding Sam's handkerchief to her mouth.

'Anybody hurt bad?'

'A split lip and some bruises. They weren't going fast. Where can I get help?'

'We're on our way to town. We could send Charlie Hall

back out with his wrecker for the car. Ed, if you want to wait here and ride back in with Charlie, I could take the lady and the kids in and leave them off at Doc Evans'.'

'I was shot in the arm yesterday,' Jamie announced.

The two men looked at him blankly. A large shiny car with an elderly couple in it slowed down and then speeded up.

Sam helped Carol across the ditch and put her in the sedan. She made no protest. There was just room for Bucky in back with the tools. Jamie sat on Nancy's lap in front. The driver got in and said, 'Doc Evans is on the left-hand side in a white house just when you get inside the town limits.'

As they drove off Sam said to the man named Ed, 'I didn't even remember to thank him.'

'I don't guess his feelings are hurt. I can't get this straightened out. Who was driving what?'

'My wife was driving the station wagon and I was leading in the MG with my daughter. I happened to look back when it happened.'

'I get it. Pretty tricky thing to stay out of trouble when you lose a front wheel.'

'Front wheel? I didn't even notice that. The front left wheel.'

'Ought to be around here someplace. Probably ran off the other side.' They found it after five minutes of search, fifty feet from the road. The chrome rim had glinted in the sun and Ed had spotted it. Three cars stopped and were waved on. Ed got down in the ditch and looked at the wheel bolts. He touched one gently with a thick finger.

'Funny,' he said.

'What's the matter?'

'Nothing sheared. The threads got chewed up some. How far you come?'

'From Aldermont.'

'Well, I'd guess you had maybe only three nuts on here and each one of those turned just enough to catch the threads. Kids act crazy these days. Even if the nuts weren't tightened down tight enough, they couldn't all work off. Crazy kids, I'd say, playing a pretty nasty trick on you. Let's see if we can find the hub cap.'

The wrecker arrived a few minutes after Sam found the hub cap in the ditch on the other side. The car was efficiently winched up onto its wheels and pulled out of the ditch. The right side of the station wagon was crumpled and two windows were cracked. Sam listened to directions about how to find the repair garage, thanked Ed, and drove in to the doctor's. The small town was called Ellendon. The doctor's name was Biscoe. He explained he was taking over the practice from Dr. Evans. He was small, dark, feline – with a black mustache and trace of unidentifiable accent. He wore a crisp white tunic.

He took Sam off into a small examination room, closed the door and offered Sam a cigarette. 'Mr. Bowden, is your wife, would you say, a nervous woman? Tense?'

'No.'

'Then has she been under some great strain lately?'

'Yes. A very great strain indeed.'

He waved his cigarette. 'I sense – you know – undercurrents. The boy's bullet wound. I checked to see if the stitches held. This is none of my business. But were it my wife, I would take steps to see the strain is ended. Soon. It is like combat. She has committed all of her reserves. She is totally in action. She could be broken.'

'What would that mean?'

'Who can say? Retreat from reality when reality becomes more than she wishes to bear, or can afford to bear.'

'But she's very stable.'

Biscoe smiled. 'But not dull stable, stupid stable. No. Intelligent, sensitive, imaginative. She is frightened out of her wits, Mr. Bowden. I have given her a mild sedative. You can get this prescription filled for her, please.'

'How about her mouth?'

'Not enough of a split to try a stitch. I stopped the bleeding. It will be puffed out for a few days. The small one is pleased with his bump. He admires it in the mirror. No other damage.'

'I have to go and see about the car. Would I be imposing too much if I asked to leave them here while I check?'

'Not at all. Miss Walker will have your bill, Mr. Bowden. Your wife is resting and your well-behaved children are out in the back admiring my Belgian hares.'

The station wagon was on the alignment rack being worked on. The service manager said, 'Not much damage. We had to use a file on a couple of those chewed threads before we could get the wheel back on. It's 'way out of alignment, but I don't think the frame is sprung. Neither right-hand door will open. We replaced the oil that ran out. Hammering it out would be a long job, of course. But I imagine you want to get back on the road.'

'I'd like to. I don't think my wife will want to drive. Can you people store my MG for a few days?'

'Sure thing.'

'How soon will the car be ready?'

'Give us another forty minutes.'

'Can I give you a check?'

'Certainly.'

After he had got the prescription filled, he went back to the doctor's. The nurse showed him where Carol was resting. The shades were drawn and her eyes were shut, but she wasn't sleeping. She opened her eyes when he approached the bed. There were spatters of dried blood on her blouse. She smiled weakly and he sat down on the edge of the bed and took her hand.

'I guess all my sawdust ran out,' she said.

'About time, wasn't it?'

'I'm ashamed of myself. But it wasn't tipping over in the car. I guess you know that. It was Jamie. Ever since it happened. A little boy like that. Trying to kill him with a gun. Trying to shoot him to death, like killing a little animal.'

'I know.'

'I just couldn't stop thinking about it. Does my mouth look terrible?'

'Horrible,' he said, grinning at her.

'You know, when I look down I can see my upper lip. It's cut on the inside. He packed something in there. He's very nice.'

'He gave you something.'

'I knew. It takes the edges off everything. It makes me feel floaty. Is the car ruined?'

'It'll be ready to roll in a half hour. It won't be pretty but it'll run.'

'That's wonderful! But … but I don't want to drive it any more today.'

'I'm storing the MG here and we'll all go in the wagon.'

'All right, dear.'

'How did it act?'

'Right from the first it wasn't steering right. You know,

it sort of wandered. I thought it was out of line gain. I had to steer it every minute. And then, on curves, it would make a funny crunchy noise up in the front somewhere. Then, just before it happened, it got much worse. There was a terrible vibration. I was just starting to put my foot on the brake and blow the horn for you to stop when I saw the wheel go scooting out ahead of me. Just when I realized what it was, we were turning over and something hit me in the mouth. Do they know what happened?'

'Somebody loosened the nuts.'

She looked up at him and then closed her eyes and shut her hand hard on his fingers. 'Oh, God!' she whispered.

'He knows the car. He would know the nearest hospital was in Aldermont. He could find that out. Aldermont isn't large. I don't imagine they have a night watchman on that lot across from the hotel. If we'd taken the main road with all that fast traffic, it might have been a different story.'

'When does all our luck run out? How long do we wait before that happens?'

'They'll pick him up.'

'They'll never pick him up. You know that. I know that. And if they pick him up, they'll let him go again the way they did last time.'

'Please, Carol.'

She turned her face away from him. Her voice was far away. 'I think I was about seven years old. My mother was still alive. We went to a carnival. There was a merry-go-round and my father lifted me up onto a big white horse. It was wonderful for a while. I held the brass pole and the horse went up and down. I didn't know until later that my father paid the man to make it a long, long ride. After a while the faces of the people began to blur.

The music seemed to get louder. When I looked out all I could see was streaks. I wanted it to stop. When I shut my eyes I felt I was going to fall off. Nobody could hear me yell. I had the feeling it was going faster and faster and the music was getting louder and louder, and I was going to be hurled off.'

'Honey, please.'

'I want it to stop, Sam. I want it to stop going around and around. I want to stop being scared.'

She looked at him with naked plea. He had never felt so helpless in his life. Or loved her so much.

CHAPTER TEN

When they arrived at The West Wind in the later afternoon, the crickety little man clucked at the damage to the car, at Carol's swollen lip, at Bucky's forehead lump. Jamie had been given firm and explicit orders about talking about his dramatic wound. He looked as though he would pop open from the effort of restraining himself, but he managed it.

Once they had cleaned up, Sam phoned the office again and told Bill Stetch about the accident and then, on sudden impulse, heard himself say, 'I know it will raise a certain amount of hell with the routine, but this is a sort of personal situation, Bill, and I'd like to take all of next week off.'

There was a silence on the line and then Bill said, 'You haven't been a ball of fire around here lately. Does Clara know what you've got lined up?'

'She's got the complete schedule. And she'll know what ones can be canceled and set up for later, and what ones should be handled. She can give you the background you'll need. Johnny Karick can take on some of it himself.'

'Okay, partner. Hope you get everything straightened away.'

'I'm going to try, Bill. And thanks.'

After completing the call, he went back to Carol's room and sat at the small desk. Using a pencil and paper to help his concentration, he tried to determine through a process of logic if Cady could have found out about the Suffern hideout. He made a short list of people who knew about it. He questioned Jamie and Nancy and they vowed most solemnly that they had told no one. Except Tommy. And Nancy was certain Tommy had told no one. He checked with the owner and by judicious use of a pair of white lies learned that there had been no inquiries about Mrs. Bowden. The phone calls had been made from the office, but he had placed them himself. Mail had been delivered directly to the office. He had posted his letters to Carol himself. The possibility of Cady tailing them to Suffern was remote. He thought back over the possible times and decided it was so remote as to be checked off entirely.

In the end he decided that Suffern was safe. With proper care it would remain safe. He knew he could not function efficiently if he based his moves on hunch and superstitious alarm. There had to be some starting place. Suffern was safe. So Suffern was an adequate base, a place to operate from.

On Friday and Saturday and Sunday they vegetated. Rest and the sedative improved Carol's nerves. They swam in sunlight, and in a heavy rain, and once by moonlight. They ate hugely and slept long hours. And slowly, hour by hour, the resolution grew in Sam's mind. He found it almost impossible to face it at first. But it became easier and easier. The concept was so alien to his nature as to revolt him. It meant a reversal of all his values, of all the things he lived by. He knew that this inner combat made visible changes in his manner. Several times he saw Carol looking at him speculatively. He knew he seemed moody and absentminded.

In midmorning on Monday, on an oppressively hot day, he took Carol away from her tennis game and took her out in one of the yellow rowboats. The sky in the east had a coppery and ominous look. A moist infrequent wind would ripple the water and then die into a waiting stillness. Carol sat in the stern in white shorts and red halter and trailed her finger tips in the water as he rowed out into the middle of the mile-long lake.

He boated the dripping oars and the boat moved smoothly along until the momentum died. He lighted two cigarettes and handed one to her.

'Thank you. You're acting weird, you know.'

'I know.'

'And this is the time to reveal all?'

'Yes. But questions first. How are you now?'

'Better, I think. I could go to pieces again if I made a good try at it. Since you convinced me we're safe here, and because we're all here together, I feel better. But not joyous. You say it's safe, but my litter of three are over there, a half mile across the water, and I don't feel really good unless I can see them and touch them.'

'I know.'

'Why do you want to know how I am? Outside of polite curiosity.'

'There's something I want to do. I can't do it alone.'

'What do you mean?'

'I've been up one side of this and down the other. I want to kill Cady.'

'Of course. So do I, but . . .'

'That was not a figure of speech. I mean that I want to plan it all out and lay a trap and kill him and dispose of the body. I want to commit murder, and I think I know how it can be done.'

She stared at him for what seemed a long time. And then she looked away, as though in shyness. 'Not murder. Execution.'

'Don't help me rationalize. Murder. And it may go wrong, but not if we're careful. Have you got guts enough to help me?'

'I have. It would be doing something. It would be something besides waiting around and looking at the children and wondering which one you're going to lose. Yes, Sam. I can help and you can depend on me and there won't be any going to pieces, either. Waiting is what ruined me. Action won't.'

'That's what I hoped. Your part is harder than mine.'

'Tell me,' she said. She was leaning forward, dark eyes frowningly intent, tanned arms crossed and resting on her knees. He looked at her and thought how good her legs were, and how all of her was truly compact and vibrant. The gusts of wind had turned the boat, and the far-off copper was higher in the sky, and the water at the end of the lake behind her looked dark. The dark water and the sky made the white houses stand out clearly at the end of the lake.

It was, to him, a moment of curious significance, of a dramatic unreality. This, he thought, cannot be Sam and Carol, man and wife. He had thought he knew this woman and knew himself. But this was a time of change. There was a new quality of tension and excitement between them, but there was an unhealthiness about it, a tinge of rot.

'Tell me, Sam,'

'You can help me plan it. I just have ... a general idea. It started with something the sheriff said. I haven't worked out the details. We leave the kids here. Nancy can accept the responsibility.'

'What do we tell them?'

'We certainly don't tell them what we want to do. We can think of something. Some plausible lie. You and I go back home. We have to gamble that he'll come there. Particularly if he thinks you are alone. We'll have to make it look that way, somehow. We can't take a chance of giving him the same kind of chance at you he had at Jamie. I've been thinking of the layout. If you were in the side yard or in the back of the house, he'd have that chance. Or clearly visible in any window in the back of the house at night.'

'Of course. Where will you be?'

'I should be hidden in the house somewhere. Waiting.'

'Won't he know that it's a trap? Won't he sense it?'

'Perhaps. But we ought to make it look good. It's the details I haven't figured out yet.'

She bit at the corner of a thumbnail. 'If you could be in the top of the barn?'

'I'd be too far away. I ought to be in the house with you.'

'If there was some sort of signal system, it wouldn't be too far. Didn't Nancy and Sandra fix up a buzzer thing a couple of years ago?'

'And got me to string the wire. I know the wire is still up.'

'I could sleep in Nancy's room. You could get it working again.'

'But why the kids' place in the barn?'

'I thought how we could make it look right. You could take the MG. Then I could go out in the wagon as though I was going shopping. I could pick you up someplace and you could lie down in the wagon and I could drive right into the barn when I come back, and then go to the house with a bundle of groceries. And we could buy food you could keep in the top of the barn. I mean that would be a way to come back without him knowing it.'

'But what if he doesn't see me leave?'

'The one car would be gone anyway, and if we did it any other way, he might see you come back.'

'I could wait until night and sneak into the house.'

'If it's supposed to look as if I'm alone in the house, the best way is to *be* alone in the house. And if he's watching he'll satisfy himself I'm alone, and then he'll come in after me.'

'We've got to be sure we can handle him.'

'I'll have the Woodsman and you'll have that new gun. There's a lot of things I can do to make sure I'll be safe from him long enough. Like stringing pots and pans on the stairs so he'd have to make a noise.'

'Can you handle it, Carol? Can you?'

'I know I can.'

'Then there's another part to the problem. Suppose we ... are successful? What then?'

'Well, wouldn't he be a prowler? I mean, can't you shoot a prowler? And the police know about him, don't they? And he is a criminal. Couldn't we just call?'

'I ... I guess so. I guess that would be all right. I thought of that road job. They're doing a lot of fill.'

'But so many things could go wrong, and then it would look bad for us, wouldn't it?'

'You're right, of course. I'm not thinking very clearly.'

'We can do it, darling. We have to do it.'

'And we can't be careless. Not for a minute. We've got to stay as cold as ice.'

'What if nothing happens?'

'Something will. He can't afford to wait much longer. He wants to move in and finish it. Shall we go back in the morning?'

'Today, darling. Please. Let's go today and get it started and then it will be over. Row back now, please.'

They left after lunch. On the way down to Ellendon to pick up the MG they discussed whether Nancy had completely accepted the lie they had told her. They made slow time in constant heavy rain, in wind that had brought branches down onto the road. Nancy had been very grave and conscientious about her responsibility to the younger ones. And she had tried to tell them that she didn't think it was very smart to go back and get the police to make a greater effort to pick Cady up. She thought it unwise to try to stay at home. She said they should stay at a hotel in New Essex. And she wished both of them wouldn't leave, but if that was the way they wanted to do it, she could certainly take care of Jamie and Bucky and keep them out of trouble.

They arrived home a little after five, put the two cars in the barn, and hurried to the house with their luggage. The rain had stopped and the trees were dripping. When they went across the lawn Sam realized he was hurrying with his shoulders hunched, and trying to stay between Carol and the hill that rose behind the barn. He felt relief when they reached the comparative safety of the front porch. He sensed that it was absurd to imagine that Cady would be sprawled up there on the wet hill, cheek against the stock, finger on the trigger, tracking them with the telescopic sight. He could not be that ready. But, on the other hand, it was equally absurd to assume that he would not be ready, and act as if he were not ready.

Before dark Sam went up to the attic window in the rear of the house and carefully searched the hillside with his binoculars. He wished it were not so heavily wooded, that there were not so many huge gray boulders, so many dead-falls.

They went through the house together, before dark, decided what areas were safe. They decided it would be unwise to use the kitchen at night. She could use the study and Nancy's room. After dark he risked going out to make certain that he could not see into either of these two lighted rooms from outside. He circled the house with the revolver in his hand, moving with caution, stopping where the night shadows were most black to wait and listen.

When he went back into the house he found he had spent too long outside. Carol held him tightly and he felt her body tremble. He locked the house with greet care, checking every door and window. They slept in their own room. Carol went to sleep in his bed, his arms around her, and the gun under the pillow, the bedroom door locked, a Rube Goldberg trap of pans and string blocking both stairways.

Tuesday, the sixth of August, was a golden day. After breakfast he checked the buzzer system, and Carol went with him when he drove down to get batteries. Before they left he checked the station wagon over carefully.

Each time they had to cross between house and barn, they moved very quickly. And each time he glanced up at the hill. He became more and more convinced that Cady was up there. And Cady would not be at all surprised that they ran.

When the buzzer system was working and had been

completely checked, they decided on signals. During waking hours she would press her toy telegraph key three times, quickly, on the hour, and he would return the same signal. She would leave Nancy's room only when it was absolutely necessary, and then for as brief a time as possible. It was evident that Cady could not break in without her hearing him. At the first suspicious noise she was to hold the key down for a single long signal.

There was no good feeling of excitement. It had no flavor of a game. No nervous jokes. The tension was grim and strong. They said no more to each other than was necessary, and they both avoided looking into each other's eyes. It was as though they had embarked on some project that shamed them.

He said, 'I think we're as ready as we'll ever be.'

'How soon will I follow you?'

'This is the part I don't like. It shouldn't be too soon. But I don't want to leave you alone any longer than I have to.'

'I'll be all right. It's a chance we have to take. It's eleven o'clock now. Twelve o'clock sharp?'

'All right.' He looked at her, wondering about her.

She touched his arm. 'It's not so bad in the daytime, really. I'll be careful, and I'll be all right.'

He kissed her quickly and found her lips cool and dry and unresponsive. He waited on the porch until he heard her lock the door. He backed the MG out, swung it around quickly and headed down to the village. He put the car in Barlow's garage for a complete engine overhaul. He walked from there to the new supermarket on the far side of the village. He bought a good flashlight and the food he thought he would need. As it grew closer and closer to noon his tension increased. The village horn blew at noon. A chill drop of sweat ran down his ribs. At five after twelve, just as he was beginning to feel frantic, she came through the front door and paused, looking around until she saw him, and came directly toward him.

'Betty Hennis,' she said in a low voice. 'I had to be rude to get rid of her. Have you got everything you'll need? Let me see.' She made a few more selections. 'I think we should kill some time, dear,' she said. 'If I've gone shopping, I shouldn't return too soon. And you should get something to read.'

He did not know at which precise moment he turned against their careful plan. He had thought they could do it. He had thought Cady could be handled. But there was so much at stake, so much that could go wrong. And the whole device seemed so totally out of character for both of them. He had the feeling that if it succeeded, it would turn their world into a jungle from which they could never escape.

'Let me drive,' he said as they walked toward the station wagon.

'What? What are you going to do?'

'I'm going into the city. We're going into the city. I'm going to try Captain Dutton again.'

Her voice trembled. 'He hasn't done anything. He won't do anything. It won't do any good. Let's do it our way.'

'I've got to try this one last time.' He smiled bitterly and sadly. 'Rack it up to my intense devotion to law and order.'

'He won't do anything, and he'll stop us from doing what we want to do.'

'Don't start to cry.'

'But it puts us back where we were. Just waiting and waiting and being scared every minute.'

Captain Mark Dutton was out, and they had to wait over forty minutes before he came back to headquarters. The waiting room was barren and depressing. The people who went through glanced at them, quick, brief glances that contained no interest, no curiosity. Carol sat woodenly, her face stamped with hopelessness.

At last a clerk came for them and took them to Dutton's office.

CHAPTER ELEVEN

Dutton greeted them with bored courtesy, They sat in two chairs near his desk.

Sam said, 'Did you hear about … the trouble we had down at—'

'A report and a request for information came in from Sheriff Kantz. There's a pick-up order out on Cady. Unless he leaves the area, he won't stay loose very long. How is your boy?'

'He's all right. We were lucky.'

'How long can we keep on being lucky?' Carol said flatly.

Dutton gave her a quick measuring glance. 'Are your children in a safe place?'

'We think so. We hope so,' Sam said. 'But in a business like this, there are no guarantees. The man is insane.'

Dutton nodded. 'From what's happened, assuming he was the sniper, I'd say that was a fair estimate, Mr. Bowden.'

Dutton listened with no change of expression while Sam told him of the loosened wheel lugs.

'All I can say to you is I hope we can pick him up soon. I don't know what other assurances I can give you. I've given the job the best priority I can give it. If you people can … be careful until we—'

'You want us to hide,' Carol said sharply.

'That's one way to put it, Mrs. Bowden.'

'You want us to hide and wait and then, when he's wanted for murder, you'll give it some extra priority.'

'Now just a moment, Mrs. Bowden. I explained to your husband—'

Carol stood up. 'There's a lot of explaining going on. I didn't want to come here. I'm sorry I came here. I knew you'd be nice and rational, Captain Dutton. I knew you'd pat us on the head and send us away full of some kind of forlorn confidence that you people will be able to handle this.'

'Now, just—'

'I'm talking, Captain Dutton. And I'm talking to you and I want you to listen. We were going to try to trap that ... animal. We were going to use me as bait. And we were going to depend on the gun you let my husband carry. I'm astonished you went so far as to let him have a gun. And when everything was arranged, he felt he had to come down here and see you again. And I knew it would be just the same as before.'

'Carol ...'

'Be still, Sam. The world is full of too many little men full of self-important, petty authority and not one ounce of imagination or kindness. So fill out all your neat little priority forms, Captain, and we'll go home and try to do it our way. Unless, of course, you can quote some law that will restrain us from even trying. My children are threatened, Captain, and if I can kill Mr. Cady, I will gladly do so, with a gun or a knife or a club. Let's go, Sam.'

'Sit down, Mrs. Bowden.'

'I don't see how—'

'Sit down!' For the first time there was the full ring of dominance and authority in the man's voice. Carol sat.

Dutton turned toward Sam. 'Just how did you plan to trap Cady into coming to you?'

'There's a lot of ifs. If I can be smuggled back in the station wagon and sneak into the kids' room in the barn. If he is watching the house. If our signal system works. If he thinks Carol is alone and decides to come after her. If I can fire at him and hit him.'

Dutton looked at Carol. 'Do you people think he's watching your house?'

'I think so. Yes,' Carol said. 'Maybe it's nerves. But I think he is. We're pretty isolated there.'

'Please wait right here,' Dutton said and left the office quickly.

'I'm sorry, darling,' Carol said. Her mouth was trembling.

'You were slightly magnificent.'

'I made a fool of myself. But he made me so angry.'

'A lioness.'

'No. Ninety percent rabbit.'

Dutton was gone for a full fifteen minutes. When he came back he had a young man with him, a brown young man in his twenties, short and stocky, with mild blue eyes and a lip that struggled to cover buck teeth, and brown hair that needed cutting. He wore a white shirt, dark-blue trousers, and a yellow pencil behind his ear.

He stood at semiattention as Dutton went around his desk and sat down. 'This is Corporal Kersek. He's restless, unmarried, a first-class pistol shot, and bored with his current assignment in Communications. Andy, this is Mr. and Mrs. Bowden. I've cleared his assignment with the County and with the State Police. Andy was an infantryman in Korea. I can assign him to you for three days, Mr. Bowden. He understands the situation in general. Go over your plan with him in detail, and accept his recommendations for any changes. Good luck to you. And, Mr. Bowden …'

'Yes?'

Dutton smiled thinly. 'You have an alarmingly effective wife. And a very handsome one.'

Carol flushed and smiled and said, 'Thank you, Captain Dutton.'

They talked with Kersek in a small room just large enough to hold six chairs, a table and a radiator. Sam explained the original plan and made a rough sketch of the house, barn and grounds on a yellow pad. Andy Kersek was shy and awkward at first but as he began to take more of an active interest in the problem, he became more articulate.

'About how far from the house to the barn, Mr. Bowden?'

'A hundred feet.'

'I think it'll be better if I'm in the cellar. I can make it there after dark. You could open a cellar window for me, Mrs. Bowden.'

'It's a damp cellar.'

'I can make out all right.'

It pleased Sam that Kersek did not in any way question that Cady would make an attempt. It made the whole project seem more businesslike and official.

After he drew the equipment he thought he would need, they drove him to his rooming house, where he changed to dark shabby slacks, a dark shirt and tennis shoes.

Before they reached the village, Sam and Kersek stretched out in the back of the wagon and pulled a dusty car blanket over them. Sam knew all the familiar turns. He felt the pitch of the hill, and knew just when she would have to slow down for the driveway. When she drove into the barn, less light came through the blanket, and the motor sound became louder before she turned it off. She opened the left rear door and picked up the bag of groceries for the house.

'Be careful,' Sam said in a low voice. She nodded, her lips compressed. He and Kersek got out of the car and he stood well back from the dusty window and watched her scurry across the lawn toward the house, through the late-afternoon sunlight, moving with all the clean grace so familiar and so dear to him. He saw her unlock the door, go inside and close it. He turned and saw that Kersek was tensed and waiting.

'What's the matter?'

'He could be inside waiting. She'd get a chance to yell once.'

Sam cursed himself for not having thought of that. They stood in the intense silence of the barn, listening. The cooling motor of the station wagon ticked. Suddenly, startling both of them, the buzzer sounded in the upstairs room – three short, quick sounds.

'All clear,' Sam said gratefully. He climbed the ladder quickly and returned her signal. It was just four o'clock. Kersek helped him carry his stuff up and get organized. Kersek left his supplies near the foot of the ladder. They sat upstairs on the old Army cot, surrounded by broken toys, half-completed projects, a hundred pictures cut out of magazines and tacked and pasted to the rough walls. They talked in low voices. Sam told Andy Kersek the complete story of Max Cady.

The single cobwebbed window looked toward the

house, and from where he sat, Sam could look along the thin wires that sagged and lifted again to enter the house through the hole drilled in Nancy's window frame. He could see a portion of the hill behind the house, but he did not try to see more of it because he did not want to get his face too close to the window.

Carol sent her brisk signal each hour on the hour. After they had exhausted the subject of Cady, Kersek talked about Korea and how it had been, and how he had been hurt and how it had felt. They both read for a time – Kersek reading at random in the great pile of dusty comic books in the corner. And at last it grew too dark to read and too dark to smoke.

Carol buzzed at nine and at ten, and Kersek muffled the buzzer, suspecting the sound might carry too far in the stillness of the night.

'Time to move,' Kersek said. He seemed shy again. He held his hand out and Sam took it.

'I don't want anything to happen to her,' Sam said.

'Nothing will.' There was reassurance and confidence in his voice. Sam followed him down the dark ladder, feeling his way. Kersek drifted out into the night. He made no sound. Sam strained his eyes to see him, but he could not. Kersek had smudged his face, and his clothes were dark, and he moved with the ease and vigilance of a trained man.

The faint light that showed around Nancy's window went out at ten-thirty. He tried to sleep, but he could not. He listened to the sounds of the long summer night, the insect chorus and the distant dogs, and the few cars on the road, and the far-off trucks, and a long, brazen Diesel hoot far down the valleys.

The first light of dawn awakened him, and he moved

the cot back away from the window. There was no signal at six, and he resisted the temptation to initiate a signal. The slow minutes passed. The hour from six to seven seemed but little longer than eternity. There was no signal from her at seven. The house looked silent and dead. They were in there, slain while he slept. At five after seven he could wait no longer. He initiated the signal. Twenty seconds later, as he was reaching again for the key, his mouth dry and his heart pounding, the signal was returned. He took a long deep breath and was immediately sorry he had awakened her. She needed sleep so very badly.

He ate. The long morning passed. A salesman parked in front of the house and walked to the front door and waited there several minutes before giving up and driving away. A brown-and-white cat stalked a bird across the lawn, tail twitching, ears forward, body crouched. It sprang and missed and looked up into the elm for a few moments, then sat and washed neatly, and strolled away, the birds scolding it.

By noon his worry over the children had become intense. If Cady had found out, somehow … But Carol had promised to call them twice a day, and if anything was wrong, she would have come running to the barn.

He could not remember ever having spent a longer day. He watched the shadows change and lengthen. At six the sun went behind a bank of dull clouds in the west behind the house, and night came earlier than usual. She made her last signal at ten o'clock and her light was out shortly afterward.

… fogged dream in a deep sleep, dream interrupted by the morning alarm clock. And he groped for the clock that was not there, and suddenly sat up in absolute darkness, his reactions so blurred by heavy sleep that for long and precious seconds he did not know where he was, nor why his heart should be hammering so heavily.

When shrill realization came, he rolled off the cot and tried to scoop up the gun and flashlight. His body was clumsy with sleep and he pawed the flashlight away from him and then found it in the darkness. He lowered himself hastily through the trap door, found the rungs of the ladder with his toes. He had not anticipated how awkward it would be to try to climb down in complete darkness carrying a gun and flashlight.

His foot slipped and when he tried to catch himself, his hand slipped. He fell and landed with his right foot on something uneven. It was an eight-foot drop and he landed with his entire weight on the right ankle. It felt as though a white flare had exploded inside his ankle. He fell heavily, faint with pain, a sprawling fall that brought him up against a wheel of the car, rolling in darkness, empty-handed, his sense of direction completely confused. He got up onto his hands and knees, grunting with pain, and he realized the long alarm cry of the buzzer had stopped. He began to paw around in the darkness, sweeping his hands across the floor, feeling for gun and flashlight.

He touched the roundness of the flashlight, snatched it up and pushed the switch, but it did not light. He heard a scream of complete and shocking terror, a scream that seemed to tear a long and ragged strip off his heart, and he heard the muffled and yet brittle sound of the Woodsman as two shots were fired.

He was sobbing with fright and frustration and pain. He touched the butt of the revolver and snatched it up and tried to stand. When he put weight on the ankle he fell again, and crawled to the wall and pulled himself up. Just then he heard the second scream quaver across the night air, a piece of silver wire stretched out to an endurable point, then snap into a silence worse than the scream.

From somewhere he found the strength to walk, and then the strength to break into a blundering run. The night was utterly black. There was misty rain on his face. He felt as though he were trying to run in chest-deep water. His right foot flopped uselessly, and each time he came down on it he felt as though it landed in white-hot coals, ankle-deep.

He fell on the front steps, struggled up and found the door and knew in despair that it was locked and that he had no key and it would take him an eternity to find his way around the house and find where Cady had broken in. That was another thing they had not considered. Another tragic oversight. But where was Kersek?

Just at that moment he heard a sound that must have come from a man's throat, but it was utterly unlike any human sound he had ever heard. It was a snarling, roaring sound, full of anger and madness and a bestial frenzy. And there was the deep, resonant bang of a weapon heavier than the Woodsman, a sound that rattled the windows.

There was an enormous crashing and clanging and thudding of something running or falling down the front stairs, bringing Carol's alarm system of pots and pans and string with it. And a jar that shook the house.

Before he could move, the locked front door burst open and a half-seen figure, wide and hard and stocky and incredibly quick, came plunging out and smashed into him and drove him back. There was a sick sense of floating as he sailed backward over the steps, and then he landed flat on his back on the wet grass with a great jar that knocked the wind out of him. He had managed to hold on to the revolver. He rolled up onto his knees, gagging for breath, and heard the pounding of running feet on the turf, saw something running toward the corner of the house. He fired three times at it, snap-shooting, taking no aim. He got up and wobbled to the corner of the house. He was still sobbing for breath, but he managed to hold his breath and listen. He heard something that moved with frantic haste, crashing up through the brush on the hillside behind the house. He fired twice at the sound and listened again, heard it recede, become fainter, and disappear.

When he turned back, his ankle folded again and he fell against the side of the house, hitting his head. He crawled on his hands and knees. He crawled up the steps and through the open front door, found the light switch in the lower hall and turned it on.

He could hear a faint mewling sound, a hopeless sound of fright and pain and heartbreak so like the unforgettable sound he had heard so long ago in a Melbourne alley that it seemed to him his heart would stop.

The sound continued as he climbed the stairs on his hands and knees. Halfway up he threw the empty gun aside. When he reached the upper hallway, he turned on the light. Kersek lay in the hallway outside the door of Nancy's room. The door was open. The room was in darkness. The endless whining sound came from inside the room.

Kersek blocked the hall. His gun lay five feet from

him. Sam had to clamber over him. He tried to be gentle. Kersek groaned as he climbed over him. He turned on Nancy's room light. The bedside table was tipped over, the lamp shattered. Carol lay half under the bed, curled in fetal position. She wore her pajama trousers. The top was ripped off her, hanging by one sleeve. There were two deep, bleeding scratches on her back. She made the endless and broken sound with each breath as he crawled toward her. When he tried to pull her out from under the bed, she fought him, and her eyes were squeezed tightly shut.

'Carol!' he said sharply. 'Carol, darling!'

The sound continued and then stopped. She opened her eyes cautiously, and when she turned he could see the purpling bruise that covered most of the left side of her face.

'Where were you?' she whispered. 'Oh, my God, where were you!'

'Are you all right?'

She worked her way out from under the bed. She sat up and buried her face in her hands. 'He's gone?'

'Yes, darling, he's gone.'

'Oh, my God!'

'Are you all right? Did he ... hurt you?'

'Like an animal,' she said brokenly. 'He smelled like some kind of animal too. I didn't hear anything. Just a sort of scratching near the door. And I found the buzzer and pushed it for a long time, and I had the gun, and then he ran right in through the door, right through it like it was paper and I fired and I screamed and I tried to fight. And he hit me.'

'Did he ... do anything to you?'

She frowned, as though trying to concentrate. 'Oh, I

know what you mean. No. He was going to. But then … Andy came.'

She tried to look beyond him. 'Where is Andy?'

'Put your robe on, darling.'

She seemed to pull herself together with a great effort. 'I went all to pieces. I've never been so terrified. I'm sorry. But where were you? Why didn't you come?'

'I fell,' he said, and turned and crawled back out into the hall. Kersek was breathing raggedly. Blood ran from a corner of his mouth. The leather grip of a hunting knife protruded grotesquely from his side, just below his right armpit. His nose was pulped flat against his face.

He crawled down the hall to their bedroom, pulled himself up onto his bed, took the beside phone from the cradle and dialed the operator.

'Sam Bowden,' he said, 'on the Milton Hill Road. We've got to have a doctor out here and the police. Immediately. Emergency. Tell them to hurry, please. And an ambulance, please.'

And five minutes later he heard the first siren screaming up the hill through the misty night.

CHAPTER TWELVE

Dr. Allisson, after emergency treatment of Kersek and after Kersek had been taken away in the ambulance, treated the deep scratches on Carol's back. As soon as she was in her own bed, he gave her a shot of Demerol that put her into a deep sleep in thirty seconds.

After he had decided that Sam's ankle was badly sprained and not broken, he injected it with a local anesthetic and bound it tightly.

'Try to stand on it.'

'It doesn't hurt at all!' Sam said wonderingly.

'Don't use it too much. Try to keep off it. But use it some. Big night you people are having out here.'

'How about that policeman – Kersek?'

Allisson shrugged. 'Take a guess. He's young and he's in good shape. He was in shock. A lot depends on how long that blade is. Better to take it out on the table. I've got to get along. Those state cops are anxious to get at you.'

When he went downstairs, favoring the dead ankle, he found that Captain Dutton had arrived. He was talking in low tones to a big man who managed to wear baggy pants and a leather jacket with a look of competence and importance.

Dutton nodded coldly at Sam. 'This is Captain Ricardo of E. Barracks, Mr. Bowden,' he said. 'I've been briefing him.'

'I talked to the captain when he got here,' Sam said.

'How is Mrs. Bowden?'

'She was on the ragged edge. Dr. Allisson gave her a shot. He says she'll be dopey tomorrow, but rested.' Sam moved over to a chair. 'I'm supposed to stay off this ankle as much as I can.'

'Apparently you and Kersek didn't handle this too well,' Dutton said.

Sam stared at him. 'If it wasn't for my wife and her little lecture, I would have been handling it myself, and it would have been one hell of a lot worse than it was, Captain Dutton.'

Dutton flushed and said, 'How were you staked out?'

'I was in the top of the barn with a buzzer alarm system rigged so she could call me. Kersek was in the cellar. The front stairs and the back stairs were booby-trapped. I'd like to know how he got in.'

'We found out,' the big state-police officer said. 'He climbed up onto the shed roof over the kitchen porch and cut the screen out of the window at the end of the upstairs hallway and forced the latch.'

Sam nodded tiredly. 'And Kersek didn't hear him and that's what cut down the warning time. And he wouldn't hear the sound of the buzzer. The first thing he heard was her scream and the two shots that she fired.'

'Two?' Ricardo asked. 'You're certain?'

'Almost certain.'

Ricardo turned to Dutton. 'We found two twenty-two slugs, one on the door frame at chest level, and one in the plaster on the other side of the hallway, about six feet high. And one thirty-eight slug in the baseboard in the hallway. It struck at an angle and knocked a long splinter out.'

'I was certain Kersek could handle himself,' Dutton said.

Ricardo tugged at his ear lobe. 'Handling a rough customer is one thing. Handling a nut is another. It was dark in the hall. Your man didn't know the layout, and he probably couldn't locate a light switch. And he was trying to move fast. This Cady probably came out of that room like a bomb.'

'I fired at him too,' Sam said.

'With the revolver we found on the stairs?'

'Yes.'

'Where, and how many times?'

'Three times in the front yard. He knocked me off the porch. He was running to the corner of the house. Then I heard him going up the hill in back, and I tried two more at long range. But he kept going. I could hear him.'

When the phone rang, one of Ricardo's people answered it, announced that it was for Captain Dutton. Dutton went over to the phone. He listened for a time, spoke in monosyllables, hung up. When he turned, his face looked older, his eyes pouched and bitter.

'We won't know how he got suckered, Ricardo. He didn't make it. They lost him on the table.'

'I'm damn sorry,' Ricardo said.

'What are your plans?'

'This isn't an easy area to seal off. Too many back roads. And maybe we didn't get on to it soon enough. I don't know. But I've established the blocks. We can't use dogs, because we can't give them the scent. I've got a half dozen more troopers reporting in a half hour. At first light we'll spread out and go up the hill and see if we can follow the track. I've got one boy who's pretty good at it. We can hope Mr. Bowden nicked him, and if he didn't we can hope we sealed off the area in time.'

'Just in case we didn't, how about putting out an alarm?'

Ricardo nodded. 'Six states. Give it the works. All right. Now, how about the press? My people have been keeping them off our necks so far.'

Dutton pursed his lips. 'It's a cop killing. Let's get a big spread. We can release mug shots.' He looked sharply at Sam. 'They'll want a statement from you, if they can get it. I can handle it, if you wish.'

'I'd like that.'

'I'll do it now,' Dutton said. 'The quicker we cooperate, the friendlier they'll be.' He went out the front door, heading for the cluster of lights and sounds of conversation by the barn.

Ricardo eased his tall, big-boned weight into a chair. He said thoughtfully, 'The relation between the mind and the body is strange. Something in the mind of the sane person seems to keep him from using the full strength of the body. Last year two of my boys tried to pick up a woman that weighed a hundred and twelve pounds. She was trying to break up a roadhouse on the Sherman Road. Doing a good job of it, too. Turned out it took five of them, five big husky boys, and after they had her under control two of them had to be hospitalized. From what Dutton says, this Max Cady is off his rocker.'

'And he's big and fast and in good shape,' Sam said.

Ricardo lighted a cigar carefully, examined the glowing end of it. 'Some people named Turner from just up the road were here and my people sent them back. Good friends?'

'The best.'

'Maybe somebody ought to be with your wife. Mrs. Turner okay?'

'Yes.'

He got up. 'Which house?'

'The next one up on the same side. Thanks very much.'

'I'll send one of my people up to get her.' He went out.

Sam sat alone in the living room. He felt dulled by all the expenditure of emotion and energy. He thought of all the things he had done wrong. A clown act. Fall off the ladder. Can't get into the house. A great man of action. Decisive. All it needed was for him to have run into a clothesline in the dark. The pratfall division. It was hard to believe Kersek was dead. Tough, competent, efficient Kersek. But, in dying, he had prevented the unthinkable from happening. There was that much.

Liz Turner came hurrying in. She was a tall blonde who concealed incredible stores of energy behind a facade of a look of languid anemia.

'Good Lord, Sam, we've been frantic. It was like a war going on over here. By the time we got dressed and got over here, we got shooed off by the troopers. The trooper that picked me up told me a policeman was killed over here and you are both all right. How is Carol? Where is she?'

'Allisson gave her a shot of Demerol. She's knocked out, but I don't know for how long. I thought if you wouldn't mind ...'

'Of course I wouldn't mind. I'll sit with her. In your bedroom? I'll go right up. Is it the man your Jamie told little Mike about? The one that poisoned Marilyn?'

He nodded. She looked at him for moment and hurried to the stairs and went up, two stairs at a time. He heard more cars arrive. He got up and went to the window and looked out. State troopers in uniform moved back and forth in front of the car lights. It was beginning to get light in the east. The rain had stopped. The trees dripped.

Ricardo came in and got Sam and had him come outside to show them where he had stood and fired at the hillside and point out where the noise had seemed to come from.

'I've got it organized now, Mr. Bowden. As soon as it's light enough to pick up a trail, we'll get going. I'll take ten men and we'll spread out. Dutton has gone back to New Essex. There isn't much chance he'll double back here, but I'm leaving one man here anyway. And here's your gun back. It's reloaded.'

Just as Sam took the gun a flashbulb went off, and Ricardo turned in irritation. 'What did I tell you press people?'

'Just a little break, Cap,' the man with the photographer said. He had a putty face, wide, blue innocent eyes. 'This is one time us Gutenberg boys get a jump on the television sharpies on a story. Every press service will grab this one. When do we kick off, Cap? How about an exclusive interview, Mr. Bowden? I'm Jerry Jacks.'

'Not now,' Sam said, and walked slowly back to the house. Behind him he heard Ricardo shooing Jacks back toward the barn.

He watched the start from the kitchen window, watched the line of men start up the hill, guns ready. He watched them until they were gone. The dawn sun was up. He went up to the bedroom. Liz smiled at him and held her finger to her lips. Carol breathed deeply and slowly, her bruised face relaxed, lips parted. Liz put her magazine aside and came out into the hall with him.

‘She hasn’t moved,’ she whispered.

‘Pretty dull for you.’

‘I’m not minding it a bit. Her poor face!’

After he went back downstairs he was too restless to sit and wait. He went out the kitchen door and sat on the back steps. The sun was high enough to warm his face and the backs of his hands.

In the silence of the morning he heard their voices before he saw them. They had chosen an easier path down the hill, the one that came down from the improvised range, past Marilyn’s grave, and came out behind the barn.

He went over. Four troopers struggled with the improvised litter. Two saplings had been cut and trimmed and threaded through the arms of two uniform tunics. Sam waited at the foot of the path. When they reached the flats they put the litter down in order to rest. They put it down clumsily. Cady lay on his back on the litter. The blunt face had a strangely shrunken look and it was the color of soiled dough. Half-open eyes were slits of opaque blue glass. In his lifetime Sam had seen several bodies. Not one of the others had looked as dead. When they set the litter down, Cady was tumbled over the side and turned slowly and ponderously to lie facedown in the damp grass. A flashbulb went off.

‘He made it halfway to the car,’ Ricardo said. ‘It was easier to carry him downhill than uphill. The car was hidden off that dirt road up there, covered with brush. A scope rifle in it, and food and liquor. One of the boys is taking it in.’

‘Did you have to shoot him?’

Ricardo looked at him. ‘All we had to do was bring him down. We started finding blood halfway up the hill. A lot of it. Look at his clothes. One of your shots must have hit him, one of those last two you fired. Tore his right arm on the inside, just below the armpit. Tore an artery open. He climbed another three hundred feet before he ran out of blood.'

Sam looked at the body as they rolled it back onto the stretcher. A blade of grass was pasted to the lips. He had killed this man. He had turned this elemental and merciless force into clay, into dissolution. He searched through himself, looking for guilt, for a sense of shame.

And found only a sense of savage satisfaction, a feeling of strong and primitive fulfillment. All the neat and careful layers of civilized instincts and behavior were peeled back to reveal an intense exultation over the death of an enemy.

'I'll get him off the place as soon I can,' Ricardo said. 'Stop by the barracks tomorrow if you can. I'll have the red tape ready for signature.'

Sam nodded and turned and walked back to the house. He walked ten feet, stopped and turned and looked at them. He looked at the body as they picked it up, and said tonelessly, 'Thanks.'

He had intended to go upstairs, but a sudden weakness turned him toward a chair and he sat down listlessly. He could hear Jerry Jacks talking over the phone. He knew he should be annoyed at Jacks for sneaking into the house, but it didn't seem important. '... that's right. Dead. And it was Bowden did it.'

It was Bowden did it.

Sam Bowden, who had wanted to throw his head back and yell at the sky, who had wanted to dance around the body and chant of the defeat of the enemy.

When he felt strong enough he plodded up the stairs to wait there until Carol awoke, and then he would tell her, and then he would sleep, and then he would drive down and get the kids.

CHAPTER THIRTEEN

On labor day the Bowden family, with Tommy Kent as the special guest, took the traditional last trip of the year on the *Sweet Sioux* to the island.

It was a warm day with a fresh wind across the lake. They ate at noon. At two o'clock the kids were swimming. Sam sat on a blanket in his swimming trunks, arms resting on his upraised knees, can of beer and cigarette in hand. Carol was on her back beside him, her arm across her eyes.

She grunted in a sleepy way and rolled over and craned her arms back and unhooked the bra part of the two-piece suit and said, 'Baste me, ole friend.'

He put the beer can down, rested his cigarette on top of it, uncorked the lotion bottle, poured it warm into the palm of his hand, and stroked it into the long, clean brown lines of her back. One of the rarest of women, he thought. Woman of grace and spirit, pride and delicacy. And once again he thought of the nightmare thing that had so nearly happened to her. A duller spirit might have survived the crime without too much emotional damage, but Carol never. It would have broken her utterly and forever. When he thought of the narrowness of the escape, it made his eyes sting, and it blurred the shape and pattern of her.

'Um,' she said contentedly as he recapped the bottle.

‘You are far too lazy to go in the water, I suppose.’

‘Uh-huh.’

‘I was cheated,’ he said somberly. ‘When I bought you at the slave market in Nairobi, the auctioneer said you would work like a dog, from dawn to exhaustion. You seemed firm of flesh, clear of eye. You had all your teeth.’

‘The price was right,’ she said dreamily.

‘But they cheated me.’

‘You remember the sign. No merchandise can be returned.’

‘I'm thinking of selling you.’

‘Too late. Years of slaving for you have turned me into a hag, mister.’

He sighed theatrically. ‘I suppose I can get a few more years of use out of you.’

‘Ha!’

‘Don't go “Ha.” It's impertinent.’

“Yes, master.’

It was the sort of gentle game they had played all of their married life. They could pick up clues from each other and go on and on, enjoying the play of invention, and making of it a game of love.

He threw the empty beer can into the lake and watched it move away, glinting on the ripples, pushed by the wind. He watched Nancy eel up onto the stern of the *Sweet Sioux* and go off in a clean dive as lovely as music.

Carol fastened the bra and sat up. ‘Maybe I will swim. You've made me feel guilty, you swine. What do you do? Swill beer and make insulting comments.’

‘You swim. I'll wait awhile.’

He watched her walk down to the water, tucking her hair into the white rubber cap. She waded in and swam out, her crawl competent and leisurely. He toasted himself with a fresh beer from the ice chest and said to himself, Moment of significance. On this day and this hour and this minute, I have come all the way out from under a dark cloud labeled Cady. I am, unexpectedly, quite whole again.

Carol came back dripping wet and slightly winded, and demanded a beer of her own. She sat beside him to drink it.

She looked at him, her head slightly tilted. 'You've got that thoughtful look again.'

'Instead of the usual idiot vacancy?'

'What is it?'

'Cady.'

Her face changed. 'I wish you wouldn't do that. I lock it in a neat little closet in the back of my mind, and you keep blundering in and yanking him out and waving him at me.'

'You asked. I was trying to detect change. You kill a man, you should change. I don't know how. Coarser, maybe. Certainly less sentimental. Less of an amiable ass loosc on thc world.'

'There is a change,' she said.

'Can you see it?'

'In me, I mean. I'm not such an idiot about myself and my tight little world, Sam. I thought it was my absolute right, my unalterable heritage, to be happy and raise my kids and eventually shoo them out of the nest and spend a dignified old age with you. I knew I was going to die some day, and would be a little old lady, white-haired and smelling of lavender, dying in my bed with my grandchildren around me. And you would linger on a few years, to give you a good chance to miss me, and then you would join me. That's what was in my mind. An enormous and infantile trust that this world was made for me to be happy in.'

'Isn't it?'

'Only with luck, my darling. Only with the greatest of good fortune. There are black things loose in the world. Cady was one of them. A patch of ice on a curve can be one of them. A germ can be one of them.'

'I know, darling.'

She took his hand and held it hard and frowned at him. 'So just this little thing is what I learned. That all over the world, right now, this minute, people are dying, or their hearts are breaking, or their bodies are being broken, and while it is happening they have a feeling of complete incredulity. This can't be happening to me. This isn't the way it was *meant* to be.'

'I know.'

'I think maybe I'm stronger, and braver. I hope I am. Because I know that everything we have is balanced on such a delicate web of incidence and coincidence.' She flushed. 'Your turn now.'

He sipped his beer and looked out across the lake. 'My turn. Okay. All that you've said, plus something else. It's like recovering from a serious illness. All the world looks fresh and new. Everything looks special. I feel enormously alive. And I don't want that to fade. I want to hang on to that. I think I was getting stuffy. I was idealizing my profession, and leaning on it too heavily. Now I know it's just a tool. You use it like any other tool. Use it wisely and it can help you. And when it's of no use to you, you take a course of action that will be of use.'

'Golly, such interestin' traveling salesmen stop here at the farm to see me and Daddy.'

He looked at her round and innocent eyes. 'Betty Lou,

it's always a pleasure to stop by here and eat your cooking.'

'Oh, *that* old stuff. You just want to flatter me.'

'Betty Lou, have you ever seriously considered having a baby?' He saw the sudden gravity in her face, saw the thoughtfulness, saw the almost immediate decision.

'I'd just love one. But gosh, I go look under the cabbage leaves nearly every morning and there just never is one there somehow.'

'Now that just isn't exactly the way you go about it, honey.'

'Out here on the farm you don't get much up-to-date information.'

He kissed her on the mouth. 'It sort of starts this way.'

'Does it? I think I might like it, then.'

He laughed at her and she grinned back at him.

'Let's go swim, you bawdy wench,' he said.

'You need some cold water, Samuel.'

They walked down to the water hand in hand. Suburban husband and suburban wife. A handsome, mild and civilized couple, with no visible taint of violence, no lingering marks of a dreadful fear.

He swam out with her, stopped and smiled lovingly at her, ducked her unexpectedly and violently, then swam for his life toward the stern of the boat, while the kids yelled for her to catch him.